Taking its cue from the Abba song 'The Day Before You Came', The Joy of Jars follows two timelines – 'before' and 'after' – pivoting on an event that changes everything.

I hope you enjoy,

Joanne /
/ pp

1

To my family and friends.

Thank you.

We have so much more time

than we think.

The Joy of Jars

Joanne Barker

Copyright: Joanne Barker

First Edition 2021

First published in 2021 on Amazon

Cover design: Scout Barker

This story and its characters are loosely based on the author's life as a single mum. They are sometimes fact, sometimes fiction and often somewhere in between.

Foreword...

The Joy of Jars began with a 5,000 word writing competition and ended with this book.

Just like Sally in The Joy of Jars, I was a single mum for many years, before meeting the real love of my life in my forties.

My creative endeavours so far, had been a play I wrote for my fellow brownies in the 1970s and a few front pages of the Birmingham Mail in the 1990s.

A former print and broadcast journalist, who moved into PR and marketing, before becoming a civil servant, I had always wanted to write a novel but was 'busy doing other things'.

When my entry was shortlisted by the single parent charity, Gingerbread, and Trapeze Books, in 2018, I was inspired to keep going.

It would be very remiss of me to promote this book as though I did it alone.

Family and friends have played a huge part in getting The Joy of Jars to this point. It's important I give credit to my partner Andy, (my real life 'Jon'), who has been with me on every page, my mum and adult children, Adam and Kate, who have read, listened and critiqued, my very talented niece and her mum who did the cover and some special friends, (they know who they are), who have supported me through my book writing highs and lows.

Finally, I would like to thank those in the book business who have helped me take a few more steps forward on my journey to publication.

Gingerbread
Gingerbread is the leading national charity working with single parent families. It provides expert advice and practical support and campaigns for single mums and dads.

www.gingerbread.org.uk

Recipes:

Pasta Bake   25
Shepherd's Pie   43
Spaghetti Bolognaise   67
Chicken in Ratatouille   83
Christmas Selection Box   95
Lasagne   117
Sausage Casserole   134
Cocktails   147
Beans on Toast   160
Chicken Tikka Masala   179
Cauliflower Cheese   197
Meatballs   217
Chilli Con Carne   231
The Witch's Hand   247
Fish Pie   255
Sweet and Sour Pork   269
Tomato Soup   281
*Boeuf Bourguignon   284

*Felicity Cloake, The Guardian. March 9th, 2017.

Chapter One

Sally was late again. What would it mean this time? Hopefully no more extreme sports or ruined furniture. Her phone had been buzzing for the last hour with demands to know her arrival time. She had ignored the messages. If they could moan, they could manage. She would find out what was waiting for her soon enough.

Wednesdays were supposed to be her short working day. It never seemed to end up that way. There was always something or someone that kept her longer than she'd intended. Sometimes she wished the world would just stop for a moment. A quick glance at her watch showed that it was still spinning at a thousand miles an hour.

She grabbed the papers on her desk and shoved them into her locker. It really needed a good tidy. Every time she opened it, something else fell down the back, never to be seen again. So much for a paperless office.

Running down the stairs and out of the door, she hesitated for a moment. Did she have time for a wee? She couldn't risk it. She moved past the toilet door and went out of her airconditioned building and into the heat of the afternoon sun.

The train was already in the station as she stood at the top of the stairs leading down to the platform. She gathered up all her remaining energy and made a dash for it.

The guard was raising her whistle to her mouth. Sally picked up speed, nearly tripping as she reached for her season ticket and raced through the barrier. She jumped into the last carriage. She could barely breathe.

She dropped clumsily onto the first available seat as the train pulled away. Keeping fit needed to move up her priority list. Yeah, like that was going to happen. And she should have gone to the toilet. Her bladder was getting really demanding. Even her own body was working against her.

In her rush, she hadn't noticed her fellow travellers. One of them attracted her attention now. And having seen him, it was a struggle to look away. He had the air of an ageing Timmy Mallet. As that thought crossed her mind, she realised half the people she worked with would have no clue who she meant. Every day, the cultural references she'd grown up with were becoming more alien to the generation rushing up behind.

Dressed in garish glasses and a brightly coloured suit, the man was tapping his trousers, presumably in time with the tune coming from his bright pink, wireless headphones. She couldn't quite hear what he was playing, as the train left the station just as it was due.

She lived only two stops from the city. And this was a fast service. What felt like only moments later, she grabbed her bag and jumped off. It was just a few minutes' walk home. Her mind ran through the sights that might be there to greet her.

Her body might be out of shape but her brain had certainly had enough exercise lately. Images of things she had faced before and those she had feared but had not yet come to pass sprang up uninvited. Yet even her overactive imagination could not stretch to the reality of what was on her doorstep that day.

The turn into her tree-lined suburban street was fast approaching. She had walked past these houses so many times before. How many residents behind those closed doors were in the same situation as her? How were they managing the challenges that brought? What other difficulties might her neighbours be quietly battling, whilst presenting a strong face to the outside world?

She increased her pace. She could not yet see her own house. But it was at about this point that she would often hear loud teenage voices coming from her garden. Today, there was only silence.

Her home seemed to have become the local youth club. Did such things exist anymore? They would certainly not be so well furnished, with free drinks and snacks all round. She didn't blame the young people taking advantage of her daytime absence. She had less sympathy for some of their parents. She had a sneaking suspicion that they might encourage a pit stop at hers before tea.

The three-bedroom semi she and her children had made their own for the last ten years came into view. As she approached on the opposite side of the road, she strained her eyes to make her usual check for trainee delinquents hanging out of windows or open doors.

She got closer, looked left, then right. No cars. She took a step forward. And stopped in her tracks.

****

The call...

Sally was in the town's multi storey car park when it happened. Her heavily pregnant body squashed into the driver's seat of her ageing Ford Focus.

She had rung the house to tell Damien she was on her way home but he hadn't answered. She tried his mobile and realised she was going to get a recorded message there too.

As she waited for her chance to speak, she was hit by what felt like an electric shock that would have thrown her back against her chair had there been any space to spare between the steering wheel and her bulging frame. It was Sharon's voice. She was saying that Damien wasn't free right now. 'Did the caller want to leave a message?'

Sally knew. As surely as if she had seen it with her own eyes.

Her growing suspicions about her husband and their mutual friend had been confirmed. She ended the call without saying a word, dropped the phone on the floor of the car and wept. She stayed like that, sobbing and heaving, for almost an hour. She would have looked a sight if anyone had seen her. But if they had, no one said.

After drying her tears and reapplying her make-up she made her way back. Damien had collected their two-year-old son, Jack, from nursery. He was making the tea in the kitchen, while the little boy played close by. Each adult made a cursory acknowledgement of the other's presence in the house. It seemed they could not even make polite conversation anymore.

She strained to pick up Jack and holding him in one arm and gripping the bannister with the other, slowly climbed the stairs. She needed to get out of the work clothes that despite being more elastic than fabric these days were still biting into her skin. Putting Jack down on the floor, Sally pulled her maternity dress over her head and reached instinctively for her stretched, worn pyjamas. Sitting down on the edge of the bed, she thought about the last time she and Damien had been physically close.

There had been nothing for months. Then, one night, she had hoped they might actually be able to salvage something. In some ways they had. The maths made it pretty obvious when the new life inside her had started its nine-month journey into the world. But she and Damien had not been near each other since. Their relationship was not just floundering, it had hit the rocks.

****

A tall, dark-haired man and a blonde young woman were standing on her driveway. They were talking into their phones. Next to them was a stocky, bald, man, with heavy-looking equipment hoisted onto his shoulder. All three appeared to be an unusual combination of agitated and bored.

She scanned the road for signs of police, fire engines, ambulances. There was none.

Surely this had to be a good sign? But why were these people here? Who were they? They looked like journalists. She had been one herself once and could usually recognise them a mile away. They would be frustrated waiting around. What did they want? Where were her children? Why had no one opened the door?

Sally approached the female first. Up close, she was both very made-up and very young. Dressed, on what would turn out to be the hottest day of the year, in tight jeans and the type of cut off top Sally had never had the courage to wear. Her cascading locks fell onto a cleavage she clearly wanted to show off. Did her mother know she went out like this?

The girl stopped talking into the mobile phone that had so far appeared to be glued to her ear.

"Sally Stainton!" she said, in what was more of a statement than a question.

"Yes. Can I help you?"

Just then, the front door opened. Lizzy stood there, squinting against the sunlight. The delighted

14

look on the fourteen-year-old's face told Sally two things. One, her daughter understood what was going on. Two, no one had been maimed in the hours since she'd last checked.

The adolescent reporter shoved a microphone in front of Sally's face.

"Your daughter entered you into a RING FM competition to find the most deserving winner of some VIP pampering. I'm here to say it's you!"

The dark-haired man, who was about her age and, although she didn't normally notice these things, rather good looking, came over to join them. There was something familiar about him. She couldn't quite put her finger on it.

"And we're here to capture the moment!" he said.

The bald-headed man was pointing what was now very obviously a television camera towards them.

She tried to process all this information, as she looked from the strangers outside her house to a smiling Lizzy and back again.

What a lovely thing for Lizzy to have done. She felt a warm glow deep inside her body. And she had won. But why? What could Lizzy have possibly said that would stand out from all the other entries? She was far too busy to be remotely interesting.

"Lizzy tells us you're a great mum." The young reporter's layers of make-up were starting to come off in the heat of the sun, revealing her teenage spots. She was a child.

"But what really swung it was that no man's been interested in you for fourteen years!"

"What?!" said Sally, in the high-pitched voice she always tried to suppress.

"Lizzy says you've been looking after them alone since splitting up with your husband. She says you deserve some attention," the attractive man quickly interrupted.

He was trying to help her save face. Even in the short time they had shared her driveway together she had warmed to him far more than the other two. Where HAD she seen him before?

"This young lady is here from Ring FM to give you your prize and we're from Look Midlands."

She was reeling. Radio and local television news? How many people would hear about this? Could it get any more humiliating?

"You're the 'And Finally'" said the bald man, speaking up from behind his camera to answer her silent question with a resounding yes.

****

The decision…

Sally kept working for as long as possible. She told herself she wanted to take most of her maternity leave after the birth. Another reason was she needed to be anywhere but at home, wondering where Damien was, what he was doing and who he was doing it with. It wasn't easy. A newsroom in the nineties waited for no pregnant woman who thought her husband might be cheating.

She was surrounded by dozens of journalists typing furiously on their clunky computers. They spent their days chasing after stories with no time to see she might have a personal one of her own. She was pleased to be left alone. She was desperate not to be rumbled as she sat almost motionless or shuffling papers in the large open plan office of the Second City Post.

One afternoon, she was given a pile of printed press releases to review and rewrite if any stacked up as a good story. Even this simple task often felt too much for her these days. Her mind had wandered to other things when the news editor suddenly barked an instruction.

"Police have raided a house in Erdington after an armed robbery. Take a photographer and go and see what's happening."

She looked up at him, shocked. Was he talking to her?

"Of course I mean you. Who else is there?"

She followed his gaze and saw that the newsroom was empty. Her fellow journalists had all left on other stories or taken their well-earned breaks.

"I can't do it. I won't do it. I'm eight months pregnant!" She was taken aback by her own assertiveness. The baby sharing her blood, her oxygen, was pumping strength directly into her veins.

The news editor stood up and puffed himself out. "Well you shouldn't be here then. Are you more reporter or more pregnant?"

Sally found she could still make quick decisions. He was right. She shouldn't be there anymore. The life inside her was more important than anyone or anything else.

The HR department was on the tenth floor of the tall office block that housed the main regional newspaper and an endless number of spin-off weeklies and supplements. The director was sitting at her desk, rifling through a pile of important looking documents. She looked up as Sally knocked on her open door.

"Yes?"

Half an hour later Sally made her way out of the newspaper building and into an uncertain future.

***

"Mum? Mum!"

Lizzy jolted Sally into action. She attempted to regain her composure. "I'd better invite you in," she said, hoping she sounded less reluctant than she felt.

Sally made coffee in her kitchen, employing her own rusty investigative journalism skills as she poured the milk and found the sugar.

She quickly discovered Chloe was a new recruit in her first reporting job. Simon was a veteran cameraman, doing freelance shifts as he approached retirement.

Jon, the rather handsome local television news reporter, took charge of the situation. He seemed to be both endearingly shy and reassuringly assertive at the same time.

"Let's film in the kitchen," he said to Simon. "The hub of the house."

He turned to Sally. "Is that ok?"

It was her least favourite room.

Simon set up the tripod and fixed the camera firmly in place.

"Can we have mum and daughter sitting together?" He put his thumb up to Jon, who nodded in response.

Sally wasn't sure if it was because she had a camera pointed towards her but she felt a strange sense of exhilaration as she looked into Jon's deep brown eyes that twinkled as he spoke.

"So, Sally," said Jon. "How much time does a single mum get to herself?"

Without warning, the french doors from the garden swung open, forcing Simon to jump out of the way. Sixteen-year-old Jack strode in confidently with three of his friends. The mud on their clothes evidence that they had climbed over the fence from the football field that ran along the back of the house.

Jack launched into his usual greeting. "What's for tea?" He stopped still. "Who are they?"

Lizzy grinned. "I've won mum a prize. She's going to be pampered because she hasn't got a boyfriend."

Jack turned red. He looked at his friends. "I don't want her to have a boyfriend. What would she want one of those for?"

Chloe turned to stare at Jack. Sally had almost forgotten she was in the room.

"We all want someone to look after us. I couldn't bear it if I didn't have a boyfriend. I don't know how you've coped for such a long time, Sally. I would have gone mad!"

Sally searched her brain for an answer that let Chloe know most people could be quite self-sufficient, thank you - as long as they had just enough money, interests and friends - without sounding like a pompous old lady.

"I'm perfectly happy on my own."

She thought she saw Jon look at her quizzically, before quickly turning back to Simon.

"We've got what we need," he said. "Thank you Sally."

She felt a pain in her side, just like the stitch she'd got when she ran for the train that afternoon. Maybe it was that wee she still needed.

Chloe wanted more. She positioned her microphone between herself and Sally again.

"Do you think you will ever find anyone if you don't look?"

Sally braced herself. This was not going to be easy.

***

The bed was wet. She put her hand between her legs. Her waters had broken. Sally shook Damien awake. He jumped up, gathering her pre-prepared bag and gently helping her into the car.

As they drove, Sally attempted to breathe through the pain. It wasn't working as she'd been promised it would.

"Hurry, hurry."

"I'm going as fast as I can. We don't want to be stopped by the police."

As they walked into the maternity wing of the hospital, the contractions slowed. Sally sat down in a chair while Damien went to the unattended reception desk.

After waiting a few minutes, he rang the bell on the counter. Still no one came. He rang the bell again. More persistently this time. Sally got up gingerly and made her way over to her husband.

He looked cross. She needed him to stay calm.

Finally, someone appeared. Sally reached out to Damien. He pulled his arm away sharply. A fleeting look of shock passed over the face of the woman who was now within speaking distance. The badge pinned to the lapel of her blue uniform said 'midwife'.

Damien turned. "About time! She's having a baby not a boil off her bum!"

He had become a Jekyll and Hyde character. Switching between good guy and baddie. Sally really didn't know which one he was right now.

***

Finally, the family was alone in the house. Jack stayed in the kitchen. Lizzy retreated to the back room to watch television. Sally broke her 'no lone drinking' rule and poured herself a glass of wine.

"What's for tea?" Jack repeated. He was keen that his mum should pull herself together and stop acting so oddly. She gave the answer she always did.

"What do you want for tea?"

Sally held down a high-pressure job. She was organised. She managed a team of people who all seemed to get on and get things done. Yet she couldn't seem to apply these skills at home.

She was a good mother to her children. They were loved and well looked after. They had what they needed and more. She gave them as much time and attention as she possibly could. However, she was a terrible housewife. She hated the very word. She wasn't married to a person; certainly not to bricks and mortar.

She was happy to make do but found it impossible to mend. She just couldn't seem to pull off anything practical. The annual task of attaching school badges onto blazers was as far as it went. Even that was a job she dreaded and put off until around midnight, the day before a new term.

Her mum would take black bin bags of washing away. The clothes would then magically reappear in the drawers, laundered and ironed. After her last promotion Sally had treated herself to a weekly visit from a cleaner. It meant getting up an hour earlier that day, to scoop up and hide all the clutter before they came.

But it was the kitchen, or more precisely, cooking, that she feared most. She felt the stress starting to build as she approached within five steps of the oven. She would rather attempt a bungee jump than host a dinner party. Simple tea times were challenge enough.

Her mum was wonderful in the kitchen. When Jack and Lizzy were at primary school their grandmother had come once a week to help out. Sally had loved arriving home to calm children, eating their tea at the table. Most weekends they all travelled to her parents' house, where they could be guaranteed to be fed, watered and entertained.

Two nights a week the children had been given tea by their father. She had to grudgingly admit her ex-husband was rather good at 'rustling something up'. The other two school days were covered by the childminder. Sally would joke that she hardly ever fed her children. Not everyone was amused.

Now the children were older and she was expected to cope. Ever resourceful, she had found a solution for mealtimes. Don't think about cooking until the moment of reckoning. Then have enough jars of cooking sauces, packs of pasta and freezer boxes of prepared meat, to get through the daily ordeal.

However hard it all felt sometimes, she was happy with her lot. She was single but she wasn't alone. The childminder might have gone and the children might be spending even less time with their dad but she had her parents and some really good friends in her team.

As Jack continued with his nightly ritual of crashing through the contents of the cupboards to find something that appealed, the phone rang. It was Jon. Her heart did something odd as he talked. Perhaps she shouldn't have had that wine so early in the evening.

Jon got straight to the point: "The diary manager's noticed that it's Single Parents' Week next week. We thought we'd do a follow up feature. Could I come back at ten tomorrow morning to interview you properly?"

For reasons, she couldn't fathom, Sally felt like she'd been asked out on a date. If she could remember what that felt like. "Yes, that would be lovely."

"Great. See you then." Jon ended the call. Sally continued holding the phone to her ear.

The moment was broken with a bang as Jack clumsily slammed a jar too heavily onto the worktop.

"Pasta bake. Please."

He paused.

"What's the matter with your face?"

Pasta Bake

Your shopping list:
1. 500g pasta sauce
2. 200g dry pasta shapes
3. 100g cheese, grated

How to make it:
1. Pre-heat your oven (200°C /Gas Mark 6/ Fan 180°C)
2. Pour your sauce into a 1.5L shallow oven proof dish. Fill the empty jar to the top of the label with cold water and then pour into the sauce. Stir in your pasta, coating well.
3. Bake uncovered for 25 minutes. Remove the dish from the oven and stir thoroughly. Sprinkle on your cheese and return to the oven for 20 minutes until bubbling and golden.
4. Ensure the food is fully cooked and piping hot throughout before serving. Leave to stand for five minutes.

Enjoy with garlic bread or salad.

Chapter Two

Sally filled the dishwasher with the cutlery and dishes encrusted with the remaining evidence of baked on pasta – it certainly did what it said on the jar. The clock above the sink told her it was nearly six thirty. Look Midlands was about to start.

She wasn't sure if she could bear to watch herself. In all her years in journalism and public relations, and despite her long-vanished dreams of being a news presenter, she had never actually appeared on the screen. It was a painful irony that this was going to be her television debut.

Lizzy shouted from the living room. "Mum! Don't be long. You're nearly on!"

Sally looked at the empty wine glass on the kitchen table. Would another mean she was breaking her lone drinking ban twice or did two on the same day constitute the same offence? After all, it had been a very unusual few hours.

There was an urgent rapping on the door. There was only one person it could be.

Josie from next door was older than Sally and had been a single mum for longer. She had started off as her role model and become her best friend. Her neighbour's unexpected arrival was a double-edged sword today though. Sally would now be able to finish her bottle of merlot guilt free. Josie never turned down an offer of wine. But it also meant she would be there to witness Sally's public embarrassment.

Lizzy ran to the front door and let Josie in. "Have you come to watch?" the teenager asked, excitedly. "It's nearly on."

Sally poured two glasses of wine and made her way into the living room. She passed a drink to Josie who had already positioned herself next to Lizzy on the sofa. She could not bring herself to sit down. She heard her name come through the television. She put her drink on the coffee table, closed her eyes and put her hands over her ears.

Lizzy brushed past her, knocking Sally's arms away from her face as she stomped out of the room.

"That was short! I wasn't even in it. I'm going up to do my homework."

Jack was standing in the doorway. Sally hadn't seen him come downstairs. He looked at his mum disapprovingly and followed his sister.

Sally had missed the whole thing.

Josie spread herself out, taking up the space vacated by Lizzy. She had finished off her own wine and started on Sally's.

"Well, I thought I was a bit out there but I've yet to tell the entire city when I last had sex!"

Sally went back into the kitchen for the bottle. She refilled their glasses and flopped down onto an armchair.

"Don't! I had to go through with it! Lizzy was trying to be kind."

"Well, if your prize is plus one you better take me."

Josie's husband had run off with his young, glamorous secretary. She had been a stay-at-home mum up to that point. She had quickly found herself a job she could fit around primary school hours, buckled down and got on with it. Now her two sons had almost flown the nest. The eldest was finishing his training as a doctor and the second was part way through a maths degree at Oxford.

"Or is this treat strictly for the celibate?" Josie added under her breath.

"Well you'd still qualify, wouldn't you?"

"Not since my milkman moment."

"Your what?" Sally spilt her wine down her top in surprise. It seemed there were still things she could discover about this woman she thought she knew so well.

**

The other woman…

Lizzy was born just as the Christmas lights were being put up in the maternity ward. She had not made an easy entrance into the world, almost as though she knew she was not entering a happy home. It had required a Caesarean for her to make her appearance. After several days on the ward, Damien took Sally home where they put on a show of happy families.

Once the festivities and new baby visits were over, Damien was around less and less. He went to work early and stayed late. Sally rarely called him to ask where he was. He rarely answered. If he did, she wasn't sure she believed him. If it went to answer machine, she would hear the voice of her competitor for his affections. Sharon's message seemed to deliberately mock her, telling her Damien was otherwise occupied and she, the 'other woman', was the only one who knew how.

The recording had never been mentioned. Damien may even have forgotten it was there. He would not have had much cause to call his own phone. He appeared oblivious to what Sally might know or feel.

Then, as the days grew longer, he offered to teach Sharon to drive. The two of them spending hours alone together. Still, Sally said nothing. She could not openly object without revealing her suspicions.

If she kept quiet, they might be able to make it through. She and Damien could pretend nothing had ever happened. Once said out loud, even if denied, her fears would crystalize into something real. She would finally have to face them.

One bright, sunny, Saturday, she suggested they got a babysitter and did something together.

"I go out to get away from you," Damien snapped. "Why would I take you with me?"

Sally recoiled. Damien looked at her pointedly.

"We've been invited to the barbecue tomorrow. You're coming to that."

The barbecue. Sharon's barbecue. Damien hadn't hidden how much he was looking forward to it. Sally had tried not to show how much she didn't want to go.

***

"My milkman moment," Josie repeated. "I find it best to compartmentalise these things and that's the box he's in."

"I have no idea what you're talking about." Sally was pleased the conversation had moved away from her and keen to learn more about Josie's possible indiscretions.

"The boys' father had told me he was marrying the secretary. I had just about come to terms with him having some kind of mid-life crisis but now this! I felt like my life was one long cliché. I decided I would continue the stereotype and have some fun myself. I suppose I also wanted to know if I could still get a man to notice me."

"The most ridiculous thing I could think of doing was answering the door to the milkman in a sexy negligee, dressing gown and high heel slippers."

"Oh my god!"

"Yes, well, how was I to know the usual milkman was on holiday? He was happily married and pretty ancient. The most I would have got was a look of appreciation. Instead, there on the doorstep was a gorgeous Adonis. He can't have been much over 30 and I was already in my forties by then. Let's just say he delivered more than my usual two pints of semi skimmed!"

Josie had finished her second glass of wine. She poured herself and Sally a third without a pause.

"But has Lizzy really got it right about you? You've been on dates, I'd always rather assumed..."

Sally readjusted herself to get more comfortable. "With my track record? That was optimistic"

"Oh, I remember! You're a marriage mender not a marriage wrecker. You should hire yourself out." Josie started laughing loudly, unable to contain herself.

Sally joined in. She had to laugh at that story. Crying certainly wouldn't get her anywhere.

Lizzy appeared in the doorway, dressed in her pyjamas and with a look of exasperation on her face.

"Sorry to be rude, but please can you be quiet? I can hear you upstairs and I've got school in the morning."

The two women gave each other looks of admonishment and swallowed their giggles as if they were the teenagers.

"Of course, sorry Lizzy," they said in unison.

***

The barbecue…

Sally had positioned herself in a wicker chair on Sharon's patio. Its big arms had plenty of room for cushions, making it much easier to nurse Lizzy.

She didn't know any of the other friends and neighbours Sharon had invited to the barbecue. Damien had seemed to hit it off with them straight away. He was running around Sharon's long, narrow, garden with Jack, as comfortable as if in his own home.

People were firing at each other with water pistols. Jack was giggling. He was enjoying himself. She could not say the same. Surely, they'd be able to go soon? It had been three hours already.

Without warning, Jack squealed. Another adult had picked up a bigger weapon. He had fired at Damien who had scooped up his son and used him as a human shield. Jack was drenched.

Damien brought the crying boy over to Sally. "He'll be alright in a minute. He'll soon dry off," he said, as if anticipating criticism from his wife.

She looked up at him. She didn't have any free hands. She wasn't sure what she'd have done with them if she had. "He's two-years-old."

"I know. I'm sorry. I got carried away."

Sharon came out of her house with a towel. She knelt to Jack's height and started rubbing him down. Snuggling her face into his neck until he was laughing again.

Damien touched Sharon gently on the shoulder; an intimate thank you. She looked up at him in a way that sent a shiver down Sally's spine.

Sharon stood up and pulled something from her back pocket. It was another pistol. She fired directly at Damien.

"That's your punishment!" she said, running onto the lawn.

Damien tilted his head back and roared with mock outrage.

"I'll get you for that," he said, chasing after her.

***

Sally was up early the next morning. She needed to call her boss. Take the day off. She couldn't pretend she was sick. She'd been on the television looking right as rain the night before. It was too obvious.

That wasn't something Sally did anyway. She was more conscientious than most people. Certainly, some of the older, married men, she'd come across in her younger days. Those who'd arrived early enough to miss taking the children to school, left late enough for tea to be ready when they arrived home, and did very little in between. Yet took great pride that their jacket was on the back of their office chair for nine hours a day.

Times and people had changed. And she'd been working in the regional government office long enough to earn a few brownie points. They came in handy now.

"I'm not surprised you want lie low," said her boss. "It's the talk of the office this morning. You'll have to hope you've only earnt the allocated fifteen minutes of fame."

He was right. Her colleagues would make the most of this opportunity. They always did. She seemed to have become renowned for 'amusing anecdotes'. Even, or was it especially, when she wasn't trying.

"They want to interview me again for Single Parents' Week."

"You really are a glutton for punishment, aren't you?"

After throwing on some cut-off jeans and a T-shirt, Sally nipped out to the 24-hour supermarket across the road. She picked up some lamb, potatoes and a jar of Shepherd's Pie cooking sauce for that night's tea. Then she walked over to the bakery section.

Once she was back home, she took the cakes she had bought out of their wrappers. She had deliberately chosen the ones that looked the most homemade. She put them in the baking tins that her mum had left from her last visit.

She turned her attention to herself. She put on some make up and pulled out her straighteners. She stripped off her clothes and pulled on her big 'hold it all in' knickers. She had gained a bit of weight since the last time she had wanted to impress but still felt good as she changed into her favourite work dress.

She told herself it was because she was going to be on television again, in front of an audience of more than a million, that she was making such an effort with her appearance. She found it harder to explain why her heart did that funny flip when the doorbell rang.

"I'll get it!" Jack shouted as he bounded out of his room and down the stairs.

She had wanted to be alone in the house. She should have known better than to mention who was coming. Jack had decided he felt ill. Unlike her he was not so averse to pulling a sickie now and then. Despite her best efforts he had insisted on staying home from school. When he had got engrossed in his latest computer game, she'd hoped he'd be as good as not there.

"No, Jack, let…" she started to protest. It was too late. The front door was swinging open to reveal Jon, his slim frame barely visible against the bright sun.

Jack eyed Jon up and down, gave a curt hello and moved away to let him in. She was disappointed to see Simon following behind. She had forgotten about him.

"Good to see you again," said Jon, stepping into the hall.

She had only really noticed his eyes yesterday. Now his voice sent shivers down her spine.

"Where do you want me?" she said quickly and instantly regretted. Where did that come from? She ushered her guests into her hastily tidied kitchen. Jack made a grunting noise of disapproval and disappeared upstairs.

Sally brought out the cakes.

"Thanks." Simon was turning out to be a man of few words.

"Did you make them yourself?" said Jon, "I'm impressed."

"You really shouldn't be," said Sally, hoping she would not be struck by lightning.

Jon and Simon soon had their mouths full. Unable to take any honest pride in their obvious enjoyment, Sally felt a need to fill the silence. "Are you married?" she asked Jon, regretting her words for the second time in five minutes.

Jon appeared not to notice her discomfort. "No. I'm a single parent myself."

Simon left the kitchen and settled the camera onto the tripod in the living room. He moved the armchairs so they were opposite each other and gestured for Sally and Jon to sit on them.

Jon looked at Sally as though asking for permission to sit down. She gave it with a wave of the hand and what she hoped was her best smile. He made himself comfortable and picked up his furry hand-held microphone, brushing some crumbs away from his lips.

"Ready?" he said in Simon's direction.

Simon nodded. Jon turned to Sally and gave what she felt sure was his best smile.

He held the microphone between them. "What's been your biggest challenge and triumph as a single parent?"

'Telling people I'd failed,' she thought.

"Finally believing I could do this," she said out loud.

****

The leaving party…

Damien had started saying he 'needed space'. He wanted to go out without her as he 'needed space'. He might find somewhere to stay for a while as he 'needed space'. A part of her was angry he would sink to using such a cliché. Deep in her heart she understood what it meant.

'I'm fine, how are you?' she would respond brightly, after the usual enquiries from friends and family. Even if she was tempted, she had no idea how she might slip 'Damien's cheating on me and I'm scared he's going to leave' into the conversation.

Six months after Lizzy's birth, she was sitting on the floor sorting gift bags for Jack's third birthday party. Both children were in bed, out of the way. Despite Jack's infectious excitement for the next day, they had gone to sleep quickly and soundly.

As she counted out balloons, badges and small toys, a plastic car rolled away from her, landing next to the video recorder. The machine her parents had given them was under the television, where it should be.

Except it shouldn't be there. It should be with Damien. It had broken several days ago and he had left the house hours earlier, saying he was going to get it mended. Sally had been upstairs changing a nappy. She had not checked whether Damien had taken it with him. Why would she?

Tears started silently rolling down her cheeks as she returned to the task at hand, wondering where Damien was, when he might come home, and how long she was going to keep pretending.

The phone rang. She heard her friend Helen cheerfully saying hello on the other end of the line. They had been close friends since sitting next to each other in a Brighton pizza restaurant, during their university's Freshers' Week. After getting a first in her law degree, Helen had moved to Brussels to work for the EU. The two women now had very different lives but would still talk long and often.

"How's things?" Helen asked, in the same way she always did. Sally answered in a way she never had before. The wall she had built between what she said and what she felt crumbled. It all came tumbling out. By the time the call ended thirty minutes later, Helen had promised to be on the first available flight.

Sally was in bed when Damien returned. She was still awake and lying on her back staring at the ceiling. She had decided she could keep quiet no longer. But she would wait one more day to confront him. They had to give Jack his birthday party first. Then she would say something. Maybe they could still sort it out. Maybe emotional wounds, just like physical ones, needed to be cleaned before they could be healed.

The key was turned quietly in the lock before the front door was slowly pushed open. As Sally heard Damien creep upstairs, she turned on her side and closed her eyes. He came into the bedroom and she could tell he was getting undressed. He used to sleep naked. These days he always kept his boxer shorts and a T shirt on. The only thing missing was a 'keep off' slogan emblazoned on the front. Although it would need to be on the back for her to see it. He got into bed, taking care not to accidentally touch any part of her body. Sally stayed still, aching inside.

The next morning Damien was up and out of bed before Sally woke. He was downstairs with Lizzy and Jack, giving them their breakfast. They were washed and dressed. He usually left this to Sally on a Saturday. He was making an effort. That had to be a good sign?

The party was in a soft play barn near to the house. A gaggle of small noisy boys had been invited. So too had Sally's mum and dad and Damien's father, Ed. Sally's younger brother, Michael, and his wife, Serena, had travelled up from London. She was glad to see them and they were happy to look after Lizzy for the day. There was also one person there she would prefer not to have come. She did not remember Sharon being invited. At least she had the decency to hang back in the corner of the room.

Helen arrived just as the party was coming to a close. She was pulling a small suitcase and still looking good, despite having obviously travelled all day. Without asking she started helping Sally to herd the children back around the table where they had just finished eating their lunch.

"Thanks for coming," said Sally, as she took the vanilla sponge racing car, that Jack had wanted so badly, from the play barn staff. "You might want to sit this bit out. That blouse is too good for this place."

Sally took the box of matches she had purposefully put in her pocket earlier in the day and lit the three candles on the car's engine. She lifted the cake over Jack's head and placed it on the table in front of him. Jack's face shone, more with delight than the tiny flames, as everyone gathered round him, singing happy birthday.

Sally stepped away to take pictures of the happy scene. Where was Damien? She looked around the room. He was standing next to a large pool of brightly coloured plastic balls, gesturing for her to go to him.

She looked back at Jack who was now excitedly watching Helen cut the cake, her expensive top already covered in jam and cream.

"What's the matter?" Sally asked, exasperated, as she reached her husband.

"I'm leaving."

"Where are you going? We're cutting the cake. When are you coming back?"

"No."

"No?"

Damien looked straight into her eyes and spoke to her slowly and calmly as if she was one of the infants in the room.

"I'm leaving YOU".

Sally felt as if she had been slapped across the face. Despite everything, Damien's actual departure, here and now, came as a physical shock. She stood still and said nothing as he turned his back on her and walked towards the play barn's exit. A song Sally couldn't quite recall hung around the edges of her brain as she noticed that Sharon left the same time.

***

"He left you in a soft play barn?" said Jon, a look of incredulity on his face.

40

Jon's question knocked Sally back into the present day. She had lost herself in telling the fabled story of Damien's departure. She always started here. Where being a single mum turned from fear into fact.

She had forgotten that story still had the power to shock. She'd had fourteen years to process what Damien had done. How he had put so much more thought into his leaving announcement than his marriage proposal. The latter made in bed one Sunday morning, almost on a whim.

And she had learnt so much since that first day as a single parent. Lessons that had kept her in control of her emotions or locked them away out of people's reach.

Her three most important rules came to her now.

1. No men who were more than friends
2. No meals with more than three ingredients
3. No more multi-coloured plastic balls

It was only the third she had struggled to follow. She could forgive herself for that. Every parent knows safely losing your small child for an hour in an array of slides and nets, whilst sipping tepid coffee out of a paper cup, is one of the best ways of retaining your sanity.

Sally noticed Simon had stopped paying attention to his camera and was unwrapping boiled sweets one after the other and quickly popping them into his mouth. There was a growing pile of papers by his feet.

She had opened her soul when she was supposed to be doing a light-hearted piece on being a single parent.

Embarrassed, she jumped up to grab the wrappers. Jon guessed what she was doing. He looked disapprovingly at Simon and scooped them up before she could get there. He walked towards the kitchen bin. Would he notice the bakery's distinctive paper bags?

"Can you use any of what I just said? I wasn't really answering your question, was I?"

"No, you weren't, but I didn't want to stop you," said Jon.

His head was turned towards Sally as he put his foot on the bin pedal and dropped the papers. "Do you want to start again?"

Sally rolled the words around in her head a few times. She looked at Jon. Her gaze dropped down to his masculine hands as he picked up his reporter's notebook. His left forefinger and thumb gripping a bright silver pen that reminded her of one she had owned a long time ago.

'Start again?' Yes. She would like that very much indeed.

Shepherd's Pie

Your shopping list:
1. One Jar of Shepherd's Pie cooking sauce
2. 500g lean minced lamb
3. 4 medium potatoes/600g
4. Small amount of milk
5. Some cheddar cheese

How to make it:
1. Boil your potatoes for about 20/25 minutes until soft.
2. Preheat your oven (190°C/Gas mark 5/ Fan 170°C).
3. Fry beef in a pan for 5 minutes until brown.
4. Stir in your sauce and pour into a 1.5L shallow ovenproof dish.
5. Drain the water from your potatoes and mash them, adding butter and milk to your taste.
6. Top the lamb evenly with the mash, cover with grated cheese
7. Bake for 30-35 minutes until mash (and cheese) is golden brown.

Ensure food is fully cooked and piping hot throughout before serving.

Chapter Three

"It's starting, it's starting!"

Lizzy's voice rang out. All eyes turned towards the television set. The opening titles for Look Midlands were scrolling across the screen.

Sally stayed just outside the room. A large stone wedged in her stomach. She would much rather have watched her interview alone. Possibly in the dark. With a cushion. Just like she had viewed episodes of Doctor Who as a terrified small child.

But she had missed the first news story about the competition. She hadn't thought to record it. She needed to watch this time. Jon had said he might call after it went out.

None of the people making themselves comfortable in her living room had waited to be asked.

Sally considered the view through the door frame. It would make a great picture. She remembered going to an art exhibition at Tate Britain. Of all the artworks created by exiled impressionists in London, one had stood out. The artist had painted all the guests at a party. Everyone looked to be having a good time. Yet it was clear he felt like an outsider. On the edge of events. He was both the centre of the picture and not there at all.

She started to count just how many of her friends and family had squeezed themselves into such a relatively small space.

Jack was loitering with intent near the french doors. Every so often his hand stroked the door handle that would enable any necessary escape into the garden. Looking just as unhappy to be there, with his back against the right-hand wall, behind the sofa, was Josie's son, Andrew. He had come home for a visit and been immediately dragged next door.

Sally's dad had positioned himself in his wheelchair in the corner of the room. He had prime position for the required television viewing. So far, he had been reading parts of his newspaper out loud to anyone who would listen. Her mum was in one of the armchairs. She was leaning forward to talk to Sally's neighbours.

Josie had arrived early enough to grab the second armchair. Next to her, on the sofa, were Rachel and Karl with a grandchild on each of their laps. Their teenage daughter Laura was on the floor in front of them. Lizzy was next to her, amusing the babies.

Sally had known Rachel and Karl since she was pregnant with Jack. She and Damien had not lived in the area long. She hadn't known anyone else who was having or had just had a baby. She had hoped attending the local group of the National Childbirth Trust would help her make friends.

Damien was not so keen, when Sally told him he was expected to come too. "You're having the baby, not me," he had said, in a tone he tried desperately to keep light-hearted. "Why do I need to learn how to push?"

Sally had persuaded him to go along to one session. He had made it as far as Rachel's kitchen. There he had met Karl, who was opening a beer and offered him one. From then on, while Sally attended Rachel's sessions, Damien and Karl would sit elsewhere in the house, putting the world to rights. It was the start of a bromance that lasted until Damien 'did the dirty', as Karl liked to say. And even though her ex-husband had fallen out of their tight social circle, the two men had stayed in touch.

Over the weeks, Sally had pushed babies through plastic vaginas and made drug free birthing plans, featuring back rubs and whale music. All of it no use whatsoever when the time came and she was screaming at Damien and loudly demanding anything that would just take away the pain.

Not that she would ever put someone off attending the NCT. It had its place in reassuring pregnant women that being first-time mums did not mean they were the first ever mums. That others, too, were just a bit scared by the whole thing. That it was ok to fool themselves they would have some control over the situation. And, unlike her husband, she did at least know what was supposed to happen.

Sally had made a friend too. Just as Damien had immediately hit it off with Karl, she found a kindly soul in Rachel, already the mother of two small girls, who would tell tales of fortunate women who had popped babies out like peas in a pod as they listened to Beethoven's Symphony Number 5 in C Minor. Their friendship grew deeper once Jack had been born. Perhaps Rachel felt less need to evangelise on the joys of childbirth, now Sally had seen it in its fully bloody glory for herself.

The two couples would spend a lot of time together. Sometimes they would take day trips with the children to zoos and outdoor play areas. Mostly they would spend evenings round each other's houses. Karl and Damien would be drinking beer wherever they were. Rachel didn't like what alcohol did to your body. At home, Sally would drink wine while offering Rachel specially bought, posh cartons of juice from her fridge. At theirs, she would be served mocktails made from scratch. Sally wasn't sure if Rachel knew she added gin from a hip flask when she wasn't looking.

Rachel and Karl had met as teenagers. They were clearly still just as much in love. Rachel was a generous, caring woman who would do anything for anyone. She was one of the lucky few who had not been hurt by another living soul and could continue to believe the world was fundamentally a good place. If she had any fault, Sally believed, it was thinking too well of people and sometimes being taken advantage of as a result.

Karl, too, seemed to take everything in his stride. For completely different reasons. Rather than seeing the world as a good place, he saw it all as a joke. Or rather the opportunity for one. He was one of the wittiest people Sally had ever met.

Sally believed it was their relaxed approach to life that helped them take 18-year-old Laura's surprise pregnancy so well. At least in public. Even when it turned out there were two surprises. When the twins arrived, they had just buckled down and got on with it. Seventeen months later the toddlers were blossoming. As far as Sally was aware, although Rachel was an expert in pushing out babies, she had been unable to push her daughter to reveal the identity of the children's father.

It wasn't easy for them. Just as they might have been thinking about getting some time for themselves, they were starting parenting afresh. Even if it was one step removed. When their younger daughter Kate had gone to university, her departure had meant the twins were given a room of their own. At least in term time. Money was even tighter though, as they tried to fund her student life as well as they could.

"Birmingham is vying to be capital of culture"

Sally's attention was abruptly drawn back to the television. The two main news presenters were running through the headlines. They were an attractive dark-haired woman who Sally had once worked with (how bad could this get?) and an older man who had already been a national television treasure before coming back to his roots in the Midlands.

"A local waterways expert has set out to prove we really do have more canals than Venice"

"And our correspondent Jon Oldman has a special report for Single Parents' Week on being mum AND dad."

She felt very warm. As if she might faint. "Who wants a drink?"

Most of the orders were for coffee. She looked at her watch. It was definitely wine o'clock. She stepped into the kitchen and poured herself a glass of cold white. Then she poured one for Josie. Her new-found celebrity status was doing nothing to reduce her alcohol intake.

"Mum! Mum! Come quick!"

Sally grabbed the full glasses and entered the living room.

Jon's head and shoulders filled the television screen. He looked good. She had to really concentrate to latch onto what he was saying. She was determined to see this through.

"The Single Parent Trust are fighting back against the stereotypes and stigma of parenting alone, with a week of high-profile events and advertising."

"I've been talking to someone who has been doing it by herself for many years..."

The sound of Andrew choking on a chocolate hobnob drowned out the rest of Jon's introduction.

Josie gave her son a fierce stare.

Sally turned on her heels and made her way up the stairs. She had consumed both glasses of wine before she reached the top.

***

The birthday surprise...

Damien had moved his belongings out before Jack's party. When Sally got back to the house with Helen, she discovered he had emptied his wardrobe and taken most of his more portable possessions.

Somehow this secret getaway left her feeling even more cheated. Films and television dramas always had a bag packing scene when relationships fell apart. She wanted her make or break moment. Her chance to either beg him to stay or to throw his best shirts out of an upstairs window.

It did not stop him returning to the house two hours later. Signalling his new status as an estranged husband he rang the bell. Sally waited at the back of the hallway as Helen answered the door.

Damien stood on the porch with a shiny new child's bike. "I didn't get chance to give Jack his present."

"I'm not sure now's the time either," said Helen.

It was too late. Jack came bounding to the door. He ran past Sally and Helen and jumped into his father's arms. Damien kissed him excessively on the cheek.

"Happy birthday son! Look what I've got for you!"

Jack scrambled down and grabbed the handles of the bike. He stopped for a moment to touch its bright blue stabilisers. He jumped on and started pedalling furiously down the driveway.

"What's that look for?" Damien asked Helen.

"As if you don't know."

"I'll bring him back in half an hour. Here's my new address." Damien put a scruffy piece of paper in Helen's hand and walked swiftly away.

***

Sally was sitting on the toilet lid in the locked bathroom. It felt like she had been there an hour but it could only have been minutes.

"What are you doing in there? You missed it all!" Lizzy was knocking on the door. "Come on mum. You have to come out. Stop hiding."

Lizzy was encroaching badly on Sally's only place of refuge in the house. The phone started to ring loudly downstairs. "I'll get it!" Sally urgently unbolted the door.

"Hello, Sally's house." Her mum had got there first.

"Yes of course. She's coming now. We just saw your story. It was very good."

Sally rushed back into the living room and snatched the phone. She did not want this conversation to continue a moment longer.

"Well!" said her mum, clearly disgruntled. "Anyone want that coffee Sally promised us half an hour ago?"

Sally gripped the phone even tighter.

It was Jon who spoke first. "What did you think?"

"It was great." Sally had no idea if that was true. She was not going to admit she had missed the whole thing. Twice.

"I hope you liked the payoff."
"Yes, yes, thank you." Again, Sally did not know the right answer. She didn't even understand the question.

Sally could feel herself going red. She wished she'd given Jon her mobile number, not the landline. Then she could walk away from the sea of faces around her. All were taking far more of an interest in the call than they were letting on. She wished even more that she hadn't drunk the wine quite so quickly.

Karl appeared from nowhere over her shoulder. "She'd say yes if you asked her out!"

"Well, I hadn't quite..." said Jon.

Sally was going to kill Karl with her bare hands. She would go out with Jon first though. If he asked.

"Of course not. Sorry. My friend thinks he's funny. He tries to set me up with every single man he comes across."

"Don't be sorry. I just didn't..."

The phone line went quiet. Sally searched her brain for something to say that would show just how much she really didn't care, without looking like she really didn't care. Nothing came. It felt like an eternity. Perhaps Jon had put the phone down?

He spoke again. More hesitantly this time.
"Would you like to meet up?"

"Yes please."

Yes please? How was it she lost all sense whenever she spoke to this man?

Sally was being invited out. On a date. Was it a date? Jon had been pretty much forced into it. She had sounded like an idiot. Most of her friends and family were watching. Was she living in a sitcom and no one had told her? Just like poor old Jim Carrey's character in the Truman Show?

Not everyone was in on the gag, she noticed. Jack was nowhere to be seen. A cool breeze was coming through the open french doors.

Jon was still talking. "I'll pick you up at 8pm tomorrow then. Looking forward to it. Sorry, got to go. It's the debrief. Bye!" The line went dead.

An hour later, Sally's mum was cooking tea. Lizzy was at the kitchen table doing her homework. Jack and his grandad were in the garden. They were looking at his road bike. It had been an expensive Christmas present six months before and always needed some kind of upgrade or repair.

Sally and Josie were alone in the living room. Josie playfully waved her empty glass in the air.

"How long has it been?"

"Since I last poured you a drink? About ten minutes. You're losing your touch."

"Since you had a date or a di..."

"Josie! About ten years, if you must know. I lost my touch some time ago."

Sally passed Josie the bottle of wine that she had positioned on the floor next to her feet. "What's got into you lately. Or perhaps you shouldn't answer that!"

Josie topped herself up. "Sorry. Can't help myself."

Sally took the bottle back and refilled her own glass. "I just can't be bothered anymore. That last date finished me off. I don't need any more friends and I've forgotten how to do everything else."

"Looks like you're bothering now. You've just agreed to a date. Tomorrow."

"I know. It's crazy. What if he doesn't like me? What if he does? What if he's not as nice as I think he is? Why do I care? I feel like I'm going mad."

"You're not going mad. You're just leaving your comfort zone. The last time you had 'conjugal relations' nobody had heard of the Spice Girls."

"That's true. As far as I'm concerned, sex is so last century."

"Stop worrying. And don't try to label everything. Giving up on relationships doesn't have to mean giving up on sex. Or reputations."

"I didn't get that memo."

"Of course you didn't. Single mums are nearly always portrayed as silly girls, sad victims or sexy bimbos. Well, nobody puts Josie in a box."

"It sounded like you were quite a successful sexy bimbo."

"We can be whoever we want to be. The secret is keeping it secret."

Josie leaned conspiratorially towards Sally. She lowered her voice.

"There's plenty of opportunities to spice up your life if you know where to look for them. Don't assume the milkman was my last delivery."

"Tea's ready!" Sally's mum shouted from the kitchen. "You're welcome to stay Josie. There are no jars in my recipes."

***

The painter…

Damien was living in a rented flat across town. Sally had not seen it. Nor did she have any desire to do so. She insisted Damien saw the children in their own home.

He denied any affair with Sharon. They were 'just friends'. Sharon listened to him. Men and women could get along without it meaning anything else.

Sally needed to speak to Damien about choosing Jack's school place. She rang his landline one Saturday morning.

"Hello?" It was a man's voice Sally had not heard before.

"Sorry, Who's that?"

"I'm the painter - doing the hall. They've just popped out."

"They?"

"Damien and his girlfriend. Can I tell them who called?"

"His wife!"

Sally slammed the phone down in anger. It soon turned to guilt. The painter was not to blame. He was only confirming what she already knew. It wasn't a big reveal.

She seemed to be set in bitch mode when it came to Damien these days. She needed it as a protective shield. Still, she was shocked by how much it stung. The reality of Damien creating a love nest with someone else and airbrushing her out of his life cut like a knife. And whilst the first cut might well have been the deepest, the others still hurt like hell.

****

Sally was determined to be ready before Jon arrived at the house. She rushed out of work and got home in time to cook tea for the children. Spaghetti Bolognaise. It was one she had mastered early on. She poured the jar of sauce onto the mince and then let it simmer while she showered. She got dressed as Lizzy and Jack ate.

"Aren't you having any?" Jack shouted from the bottom of the stairs.

"Not tonight. I'll eat later."

She was leaving Lizzy and Jack in charge of each other. She read them the riot act and phoned Rachel to ask her to keep an eye out from her house across the road. The children had finished their tea and moved into the living room to watch television.

"You can trust us," said Lizzy.

Jack scowled. "Don't know why you're bothering though. You've been on the telly now. Why do you need to go out with him?"

"Don't be mean," Lizzy replied, seating herself on a large cushion on the floor.

"It's all your fault. Entering mum into that stupid competition."

Sally grabbed Jack's arm as he moved to pull the cushion from under Lizzy. "Stop arguing. I've said I'll go, so I'm going."

Sally sat down with them and waited. She felt like a teenager again. Not the self-confident woman she believed herself to be.

The doorbell rang. Lizzy ran into the hall. Jack turned up the television.

A head appeared around the door frame. "It's only me. I've come to wish you luck."

Sally felt both relieved and deflated at the sight of Josie. She stood up and ushered her into the kitchen.

The dirty plates and left-over tea were still on the table. Should she quickly have something now? Just in case? Her nervous stomach gave her no option but to go without. She used the reflection from the glass splashback above the hob to put on another layer of lipstick. It never stayed there long. What would last longer, she wondered. This shade of red or her date with Jon?

"Is it too late to cancel?"

Josie snorted. "Don't be silly. Just get yourself out there and have some fun. Even if it doesn't work out with Jon. Once you get started you won't be able to stop."

"Sounds like you're talking from experience again."

Josie made an exaggerated attempt to check if anyone else was listening. Just as she opened her mouth to speak, a second loud chime rang through the house.

Sally looked at the clock. It was 8pm, precisely.

Josie gave Sally the thumbs up, then went into the living room and started talking to Lizzy. Sally grabbed her bag from the table, shouted goodbye and went out the front door, closing it behind her as quickly as she could.

Jon was standing at the bottom of the porch step, his deep brown eyes at the same level as Sally's.

"You've dressed up. Sorry, I've come straight from work."

Jon was wearing an office suit and tie that had seen better days. Sally was in her smartest jeans and favourite top. Her heart fell. Maybe this WAS just a fake date because he had been too kind to decline on the phone.

They walked down the driveway in silence. Jon opened the door of his Ford Mondeo. Sally got in and took in the shiny interior. He certainly looked after his car's appearance. Hadn't he said he had a child? It was spotless. Perhaps he never saw them. Jon got in beside her and smiled disarmingly. Her heart did that funny skip again.

"I was thinking Penny's if that's ok with you," he said.

Penny's was a small, boutique wine bar in the centre of town. Sally had not been there for a long time. Inside were cosy booths with waiter service, where romancing couples could hide away from the rest of the world.

After a ten-minute drive, they pulled into the car park and walked the short distance to the heavy main door. Through the glass, Sally could see there were still a couple of booths available.

Jon grabbed the handle and hesitated. "It's such a warm night. Do you want to sit outside?"

They went back through the car park and chose a table in the wide but short rear garden running alongside the canal.

Sally watched Jon from behind as he went inside to the bar. He was right. It was warm.

Just minutes later he returned, carefully balancing a bottle of wine, two glasses and a pint of lager in his hands. He placed them on the table and sat down on the opposite bench.

"It's been thirsty work today," he said, as if by way of explanation, raising his lager to his lips and taking a long swig.

He put the glass back down and looked at Sally curiously. "Are you alright?"

She had been staring. How much time had passed? Just a few seconds? Minutes? She had no idea.

"I was just thinking how unfair it is that you know so much about me and I know so little about you."

As she often said to her friends, she didn't work in public relations for nothing. Sally was impressed with how she had dodged that one.

"Oh. I'm very boring. I think that's why my partner left me. She wanted more from life than being with us. Me and my daughter, I mean."

"Anyway, we seem to be managing ok. I'm lucky I've got a great relationship with Beth. Fortunately, she shares my nerdy interests."

"What kind of interests?"

"I'm not sure I want to tell you on a first date."

"I'm worried now."

"Steam trains! There you go, I've admitted it. We love them. We've been on nearly every heritage line there is."

"Well, I don't think that's too bad. At least you get a day out."

"And magic. Mainly card tricks"

Jon was doing his best to prove his ex-partner right. Yet Sally didn't find him boring at all.

"I could show you a trick or two." Jon's eyes were twinkling again as he spoke. Either that or the wine was starting to have an effect on her empty stomach. Whichever it was, she seemed to be under his spell.

Sally picked up her glass and tipped it back. "Really?" she asked, in a way that was intended to be alluring but may just have sounded a bit too keen. "And how might you do that?"

Jon was fumbling in his pocket. "I always carry something with me just in case."

Sally's hand instinctively went to her phone. That was short lived. Was Jon really just like all the rest?

He lay a pack of playing cards on the table in front of them.

"The magic only works if we are truly in tune with each other."

Sally poured herself another glass and downed it quickly. Jon didn't seem to notice. He gave her the pack and invited her to split it, giving the top half back to him. He fanned his cards out and pushed one forward, indicating she should do the same.

She looked around. No one was paying attention to the couple who appeared to be playing cards on their night out. Although it was probably a first for Penny's.

Jon was getting into his stride.

"Now you take my card and I'll take yours and we'll put them on the top of each others' packs. Wouldn't it be amazing if we had not only selected cards of the same colour but of the same value? What are the chances of that? Let's have a look. You turn your top card over and I'll turn mine.

She saw the top card was the ace of spades and Jon's was the ace of clubs. It was an impressive trick.

"Not bad, eh?" said Jon, who was clearly enjoying the role of entertainer. "But wouldn't it be even more incredible of we could find the other two?"

Sally laughed, genuinely unable to see how he'd done it when this time the red aces were revealed. She had been looking at his hands the whole time.

"I can see you're impressed Sally. But there's more."

Jon took the remaining cards back from Sally, his nimble fingers briefly touching hers as he did so. He spread the cards out in front of her. They were all completely blank.

Jon's brown eyes met Sally's gaze.

"Are you sure we haven't met before?"

He could do magic. He could have anything his heart desired.

****

The burn…

Sally had to go back to work. She had been due to return two weeks after Jack's birthday party. She had stretched out her maternity leave for another month instead, but she could not put off the inevitable.

Her immediate boss was one of the more sympathetic news editors. That was something at least. Her base was changed to a small office on the edge of the city and nearer home, to reduce her commute. However, she could not push it too far. They would only be prepared to accept so many stress related sick notes. She didn't want to find out just how many.

Seven am starts meant leaving the house while they were still asleep; someone else being the first person they saw that day. Four pm finish times meant coming home to the children when they were ready for a bath and bed. It was made worse by needing to work weekends and evenings, sometimes unexpectedly when a big news story broke. She barely got to see them awake, alert and happy. If they had been old enough to make the point, they could have said the very same about her.

Twice a week, Damien came round to give the children their tea. He took great pride in pointing out he was giving her a break, although he wasn't prepared to extend that to weekends. In reality, it meant she saw even less of Lizzy and Jack and had to find somewhere else to go after a busy and tiring shift. Her friends often took her in for a couple of hours, where she would thank them by falling asleep on their sofa.

At least the nights Damien cooked, it meant she didn't have to, It was funny what you missed when someone left. She had expected it to be the companionable evenings in front of the television. But they had been so difficult – or absent – for such a long time. She enjoyed her few hours of peace when the children were in bed; without fear of an argument or stony silences. Instead it had been Damien's skills in the kitchen. Credit where it was due. He had always looked after the domestic side of things. It was probably one of the characteristics that had attracted her to him. Housekeeping had never been her strong point.

She hadn't really noticed while Helen was staying. Everything had gone by in a blur. But when she returned to Brussels it was clear she had been picking up where Damien had left off.

"What's for tea, mummy?" Jack had asked the first evening Sally was truly alone with the children.

She didn't know.

"What do you want for tea, Jack?"

"Fish fingers, beans and chips. Like Daddy does."

Surely that couldn't be too hard. At least Jack had chosen one of his dad's 'lazy day' meals. She found three fish fingers and a half empty bag of oven chips in the freezer. There was a tin of beans in the cupboard. She could do this. And she would have a frozen Indian ready meal. Sorted. What could possibly go wrong?

She put the fishfingers under the grill and all the chips and the takeaway in the oven. The beans tin did not have its own ring pull. She found their rusty tin opener. It had cut around half the lid when it broke in half. The bladed edge fell. She instinctively reached out. It was too blunt to work but still sharp enough to cut flesh. Great. She ran her finger under the tap. It needed a plaster. Where were they?

She went into the bedroom. No luck there. What about the bathroom? When had she used them last? Jack had fallen and hurt his knee when they were in the park. She had plasters then. The child friendly Disney ones he loved so much. She looked in the big nappy bag she took everywhere. At last. Donald Duck had saved the day.

"Mummy! The kitchen's smelly!"

Sally ran back in. Black smoke was billowing out from under the grill. She grabbed her oven gloves and pulled out the tray. The fish fingers were burnt to a crisp. Jack looked miserably at his mum.

"Daddy's don't look like that."

"Chips, with lots of tomato sauce! That'll be nice!"

She opened the oven. It was still stone cold. She had forgotten to turn it on. And she had left the plastic film lying loose on the top of the ready meal. As she reached for the cartons with the oven gloves she didn't need, she knocked them over, tipping rice and chicken korma all over the uncooked chips.

She closed the oven door. Sat down on the kitchen floor and put her head in her hands. Lizzy, who had been fed from a jar and gone to sleep, started crying upstairs.

Jack put his arms around Sally's head. "I like McDonalds, mummy,"

McDonalds? It would do for tonight. But she had to find another way.

It was a struggle to keep going. She had to keep going. As she tried to hold it all together, Sally would see 'lazy single mums' derided by the very profession she worked in. Where were the stories about lone parents like her, working till they dropped, cleaning the kitchen floor at midnight, waking alone at three am to their children's cries?

***

It had gone dark while they were talking. It was much cooler too. Sally hadn't really noticed until Jon started to put his jacket on.

"Probably should get back," he said. "Babysitter."

They stood up to leave. Sally had made a big mistake. She really should have had something to eat before she came out. The evidence on the table was irrefutable. There were two empty pint glasses. Only one wine glass had been used all night. An empty bottle was standing next to it.

"Are you ok?" Jon asked, just as he had at the start of the evening. "Oh God. Did you think we were eating? I thought we said drinks. I get out of work so late sometimes. I had a sandwich on the way."

Sally held onto the back of a chair to steady herself. She looked for a quick way out of the pub garden but the ground seemed to be rising in front of her. Even the furniture refused to stay still.

"Yes, yes. I'm fine. I just got up too quickly."

Jon started gently guiding her towards the exit. "Let's get you home."

How had she let this happen? She had been enjoying herself. She had not wanted to spoil things. To interrupt the evening. Now she was in trouble.

Jon took hold of Sally's hands. They were shaking.

"Are you going to be sick?"

Sally nodded. There was no point in any more deception. Things were too desperate.

"Quick then. Round here." Jon led Sally to the far side of the wine bar. Directly in front of them was a set of bollards around a large hole in the ground.

Jon supported Sally as she heaved her night's intake of drink into the roadworks.

Spaghetti Bolognese

Your shopping list:
1. 500g jar Bolognese sauce
2. 500g minced beef
3. 300g spaghetti

How to make it:
1. Heat a large saucepan and add the minced beef stirring with a wooden spoon until it browns.
2. Tip in the jar of Bolognese sauce and heat until simmering. Lower the heat and cook gently for 20 minutes, stirring occasionally.
3. Meanwhile, cook the spaghetti in boiling water for 10-12 minutes, according to pack instructions. Drain thoroughly, share between four warmed plates and top with the Bolognese sauce.

Serve with grated cheese on top, to taste.

Chapter Four

So this was what complete humiliation felt like. Sally was sitting on the pavement. Jon was standing next to her. Despite her best efforts to wipe it off with her sleeve when he wasn't looking, she could see a speck of sick on the toe of his shoe. Had she ruined everything?

As if reading her mind, Jon crouched down so that his head was at the same level as hers. He held onto her shoulders. Whether this was intended to comfort, or simply to stop himself from falling over, wasn't clear.

He looked straight into her eyes. "I won't hold this against you. Please don't worry."

Sally reflected that he wouldn't be holding anything against her that night. If ever. Vomit was not a known aphrodisiac.

"Shall I get you a taxi home?" Jon was good at answering questions she hadn't asked. "I need to get back to my daughter. Her babysitter doesn't like to stay too late on a school night. It's just your house is in the opposite direction to mine. And this has rather delayed me. Only if you think you'll be ok, of course."

Sally nodded. Right now she just wanted to be home, alone.

Jon stood up and stuck out his arm. "Taxi!"

A passing cab stopped almost immediately. Jon helped Sally into the back, waved her off and turned in the direction of his car.

She leant back into the padded seat. She was relieved to be on her own. Now she could properly assess the damage. Physical and emotional. Jon had been kind. But he had not taken her home. Was what he had said about the babysitter true? Most of the night had gone well. Or was it a white lie? Had he wanted to escape the situation just as much as she had? Had he wanted to get away from HER?

The taxi slowed before pulling up outside her house. She stepped out hesitantly. The nausea which had been made worse by the movement of the car started to subside.

Her phone let out the familiar beep of a text. She pulled it out of her bag, nearly dropping it on the floor as she did so. Her heart fell.

Hi Sally. Thank you for this evening. I can't see you again

Well that was it then. She could hardly blame him. Another beep rang out.

*this week. Would you like to go out next Saturday? There's a new restaurant we can try. x

Sally's heart rose again. It rested slightly higher than it had been for some time.

***

The play…

Sally had decided to go straight home. Damien might still be giving the children their tea. There was another hour to go before he would expect her arrival. But she was shattered. It had been a hard day at work. She wanted to see her children. She didn't care if he was inconvenienced. She'd had more than her fair share of disrupted plans.

She put her key in the lock. As she pushed the door open, there was a commotion at the end of the hall. Someone or something flashed in front of her and then disappeared from sight.

"Hello, only me." she said.

"I'm in the kitchen!" There was a note of urgency in Damien's response.

"Mummy!" Jack shouted, unseen.

Her son appeared in the hall and ran towards her before she had chance to put her bags down. She only just caught him as he leapt up into a hug. His happy cry washing away the trials and tribulations of the day. She carried him down the hallway. The living room door seemed to have something wedged behind it. She had to squeeze through with her wriggling load.

Lizzy was sitting on the floor, surrounded by cushions. Sally instinctively checked that Damien had positioned their daughter safely. He had. Good. Then she saw it. The fake Gucci handbag. Tucked between the side of the settee and the french doors.

"You can come out now," she said.

Sally shifted Jack in her arms and twisted her body. Just in time to see Sharon step out from behind the door. Her husband's girlfriend stood there for a moment looking sheepish. It was as though they were all starring in an end of the pier farce. Waiting for the gasps and laughs before they moved onto the next scene.

Today's performance over, Sharon grabbed her bag and walked out of the house. Pulling the door closed behind her as she did so.

Jack looked at his mum, the cogs of his little brain trying to work out what had just happened. He was distracted by the television where the Fat controller was talking to Thomas.

Damien came into the room with two small plates of steaming food. He didn't look at Sally, focussing instead on his children.

"Homemade fishcakes and carrots," he said in a forced sing song voice. "Eat it all up for Mummy. Daddy has to go."

Sally wished she had a great line for this moment. Nothing came.

***

Sally was sitting at her desk at work. It had been touch and go whether she would make it in and she wasn't sure she'd made the right call. She was unable to focus. Her head was still hurting from the night before. And it wasn't just the alcohol that was causing her pain.

She looked at her long list of emails. Clicked on the top one, opened it, read what it said and closed it again. She realised she had not absorbed its contents and repeated the exercise. After opening the same email five times without achieving anything, she got up to make herself a cup of tea.

Her boss and the Head of HR were huddled together conspiratorially in the open plan kitchen. Had they somehow found out what had happened last night? They'd only just stopped talking about her appearance on Look Midlands. Had her vomiting outside Penny's been captured on CCTV? Or more likely on someone's mobile phone? Had it gone viral?

Sally tried to keep her tone as lighthearted as possible as she cut into their conversation.

"Are you talking about me?"

"No." said the HR boss, a woman in her forties who Sally liked a lot. "Why? What have you done now? Paranoia. Always the first sign of a guilty conscience!"

"Nothing. Sorry. Carry on." Sally turned her back to them and quickly grabbed a mug and a tea bag from the cupboard. She made herself a drink, using the less than boiling water from the modern hot taps that she was sure would one day give them all some horrible disease, and started to walk away.

Her boss positioned herself between Sally and the path back to her desk. "We WERE talking about you actually,"

Sally felt the blood drain from her face. Her boss carried on.

"I've got someone to introduce to you. She's our new legal hot shot. A contractor. I've just discovered you two know each other."

Sally looked around. She could see no new faces.

"Helen Howard. She says you go way back."

Helen? Helen was here? Helen was working HERE?

"You do know her, don't you? There can't be another Sally Stainton!"

"Yes. I know her. I'm just so surprised. What's she doing here?"

"You mean why would as highflying and successful a lawyer as her come and work for us? We are Her Majesty's Government, you know. Although, to be fair, I'm asking myself the same question. We only have her for four months. Unless we can persuade her to stay longer."

Sally returned to her desk. She restlessly looked at her inbox again. She skipped over the first email which she had finally established was asking whether she had completed some admin task she didn't understand. The next three were from the media. She should reply to these immediately. She ignored them and read the fifth one first.

Hi Sally,

I'm starting a new consultancy job in Birmingham today. Only got it on Friday.

It's occurred to me it might be where you work! I drift off sometimes when you talk about UK regulations. :)

Not that European law is much more exciting. And if I am joining you, I need to start paying attention sharpish.

I hope you don't mind if I'm suddenly behind the next pot plant!

Helen. xx

So, it was true. Helen was somewhere in this building. Not across the channel, on the continent. She had always said she would never come back. Sally had understood that. Who would give up sun filled squares – surely even Belgium had better weather than here - and short hops to France and Germany?

Now Helen had swapped lunch breaks in Brussels for Birmingham. What could have led to this sudden change of mind? Sally was keen to see her friend. It didn't matter how long it was between catch ups, it always felt like just a couple of days. It was weird but wonderful that they would be working together.

She would invite her back tonight. But what would she cook? Helen was well aware of Sally's culinary limitations. She would try to decline a meal. But she was always such a good host when Sally and the children visited her Belgian flat. Sally would insist. Perhaps they could eat out? Jack and Lizzy would love that. Especially Jack. Any excuse to put off his homework.

Hi Helen, Fancy you working here. Can't believe it! Come and find me. I'm by the photocopier on the 1st floor. Come back to mine for tea tonight. Something simple!

Sally. xx

Now she really couldn't concentrate. She turned to her other emails. An online news site was asking what regulations covered sex aids. A news agency wanted to know if sausage rolls could legally be sold in inches rather than centimetres.

Sally had grown used to the bizarre enquiries that would come into the press office. Some days she found them amusing. This morning she would have preferred a job more ordinary.

Sally searched for the sex aids website. This was a mistake. The words *DO NOT ENTER!* came onto her screen, with a warning that she was violating government digital policy. She would have to send an email to the IT team, explaining why she was trying to access what had been categorised as a porn site. Otherwise, she would be put on the naughty list and called in to see the Big Boss.

She began typing. She was about to press send when she paused to attach the website's enquiry for extra back up. Her phone rang inside her bag. Something instinctive told her it was important.

"Mum?" It was Jack. He was off school again. This time for a teacher training day.

Sally was torn between mild irritation that she was being pulled in so many different directions at once and worry about why Jack might be ringing her at work this time.

"What's the matter?"

"Did you like that big vase in the living room?"

Sally took a deep breath. "Step away from the glass, Jack."

Sally wanted to shout at him. Tell him how much she HAD liked that vase and how much it had cost. But it was an open plan office. The regular phone calls from her children had become part of the workplace entertainment. There was no one else to deflect the domestic crises to when she was working. She had to just deal with them and move on.

She reminded him yet again where the dustpan and brush were kept. Maybe not very kindly. She might even had hissed her words at him. He abruptly put the phone down.

"Problems?"

"Just Jack!" said Sally, her delight in seeing Helen changing her mood.

The two women hugged. Laughing, they pulled apart.

Sally studied her friend. She looked different somehow. "Sod this," she said. "Let's get cake."

***

The plates...

"Where are your dishes?" Sally's mum pulled her head out of a kitchen cupboard and looked enquiringly at her daughter.

"What do you mean?"

"It's a fairly straightforward question, dear. I've been noticing your plate population has been diminishing but today it's reached a tipping point. There are five of us and four plates."

Sally looked in the cupboard. Her mum was right. She used to have about ten. Three had survived her university days, four were a wedding present, given as part of a set, and a few more were cheap white ones from the local home furnishings store. Only the ones from the dinner service remained. Where could the others possibly be? She checked the dishwasher. They weren't in there either.

"Well if we don't know, there's only one other person who might. Damien."

He answered the phone on the second ring. Sally got straight to the point.

"Oh yeah. They're here. I'll bring them round next time. I like to plate a meal up for Sharon."

***

The two women each grabbed a doughnut from the office kitchen and sat down. They ate in hurried silence. Neither able to talk and stop the jam from dripping on their work clothes. Sally finished first. She licked the sugar off her fingers and for the second time in a few days was poised to use the skills of her former life.

Just as Sally opened her mouth to launch into her first question, Helen was pulled away by a colleague, in order to join a workshop inducting new recruits in the ways of the civil service. Sally was relieved her own afternoon would feature only unhappy journalists and a telling off from IT.

On the way home Sally stopped at the local shop. Helen had emailed later that afternoon and accepted her offer of dinner. Despite her initial caution, Sally had decided to cook one of her more adventurous meals. She spotted what she needed. A tin of ratatouille. She picked up four chicken breasts and some potatoes She had just enough room left in her basket to add some red wine that was on special offer near the checkout.

Helen had gone back to her hotel first. Sally was glad of the extra time to warn Jack and Lizzy. Not that she needed to worry about that. They were always pleased to see Helen. She was part of their extended family.

All Sally had to do was put the chicken in a casserole dish, pour on the ratatouille and pop it in the oven. Then she peeled the potatoes and put them in water on the hob.

Helen arrived, just as she was tidying up the living room. They started eating as soon as the pleasantries were over. Jack tucked in as though his mum had starved him for a week.

"That was nice," said Jack.

"You're just saying that because you broke her vase," said Lizzy.

"It was an accident!"

"You do need to be more careful Jack. Am I really still not allowed to have nice things?"

"Well it was a lovely tea," interrupted Helen. "Thank you."

They all stayed sitting round the dining table. Sally cleared the plates away to the kitchen worktop. The washing up could wait.

Now the cooking was over she was able to relax. The wine was probably helping too. Sally had been surprised when Helen had declined but had decided she could go ahead anyway. She wasn't the only adult in the house so was it really lone drinking?

"Can I get you anything else, Helen? A coffee? Tea? Are you sure about the wine?"

"No thank you. I best get going soon. I'm pretty tired to be honest."

Sally studied Helen's face. She did look a bit peaky. And she still hadn't properly explained why she was working back in England.

"Jack? Lizzy? Do you mind giving me and Helen some space to chat, please?"

"Are you going to tell her about your boyfriend?" said Jack. He scowled as Lizzy thumped him. They started to wrestle without moving from their seats.

"Out!" Sally shouted, pointing at the door.

The children left the table. Sally saw Jack make a face at Lizzy as they left.

"A boyfriend?" said Helen. "I want to hear about that. It seems to be a day for news. There was something I was going to tell you too."

"You first," said Sally.

Helen wasted no time. "I've decided to have a baby. By myself. I can't wait any longer for the perfect partner. Or even an imperfect partner. That's why I've come back."

First Josie. Now Helen. Sally wondered how many more times she would have to question how well she knew people.

Helen filled the silence. "You're my inspiration. You've done so well on your own."

Now was not the time to point out how very hard it had been. Helen surely knew anyway. "A baby? When? How?"

"In six months. Sperm donor. Worked first time."

* * *

The soothing...

"Let me take her for a bit. You drink your tea."

Rachel held out her arms for Lizzy. The little girl returned the gesture. It was clear she liked her mum's friend almost as much as Sally did. She had spent a great deal of her first weeks and then months being swapped between their laps.

The value of good friends had shone through since Damien left. Sally had not known what to do with herself at first. She struggled to keep her head above water alone at home. She had gone to her mum and dad's as much as possible. But she couldn't be there all the time.

And she didn't want to weigh them down with all her worries. She needed a little help from her friends.

She had talked a lot. Once she started, it was hard to stop. She was haemorrhaging emotions. Feelings and fears had been pouring out of her almost non-stop. Rachel had patiently listened, offering an ear and occasional words of wisdom, letting Sally and the children occupy her home for hours on end.

As each day passed, she was growing stronger. The flow of words was slowing down. She had time to take a breath and look up.

***

Sally and Helen were standing in the hallway. Helen had brought one of her collection of beautiful, expensive, shawls and had wrapped it around her shoulders. It was still so warm, Sally wasn't sure she would need it tonight. But it was a 'nice thing'. Helen should enjoy those while she still could.

She opened the front door and Helen stepped out. A taxi was waiting at the kerb.

"Oh, I'm sorry Sally. I'm so self-obsessed! You haven't told me about your boyfriend."

The cab driver honked his horn.

"There's very little to tell! You get going."

"Well, if you're sure."

"Of course, I'm sure. We're going to be seeing quite a lot of each other from now on."

Helen got into the taxi, waving as it drove away. Sally turned back towards the house. Josie sailed past, a bottle of wine in her hands. It was clear where she was going.

"I've already had almost a bottle to myself tonight. I can't drink anymore!" Sally pleaded.

"No, no, no. You don't escape that easily. I can't go to bed without knowing how your date went."

Josie went straight into the kitchen and simultaneously poured and drank whilst filling the dishwasher.

"So, come on. Tell all!"

"It was the best and the worst date I've ever been on."

"What does that mean?"

"I really liked him and then I disgraced myself."

"What did you do?"

"I was sick all over his shoes."

"Is that all? Seriously, if he likes you what does it matter? If he doesn't like you what does it matter? If he likes you but thinks you're a walking disaster, then at least he got to find out early."

"So, you don't think I'm a terrible person?"

"That depends."

"On what?"

"On how new his shoes were!"

Chicken in Ratatouille

Your Shopping List:
1. 4 chicken breast fillets
2. One tin of ratatouille
3. Mashed potato

How to make it:
1. Put the chicken and tinned ratatouille in a casserole dish
2. Cook for 1.5 hours in the oven at 180^0C

Serve with mashed potato

Chapter Five

The ghost of Christmas past…

Sally lay in bed staring into the darkness. She looked across at the LED digits on her alarm clock. It was six am on Christmas Day. A dark cloak of loneliness hovered over her bed. It threatened to envelop her so tightly she might never escape. She jumped up and turned on the light.

Leaning over to switch on the radio, she returned to the middle of her big, empty bed. The cheerful DJ and happy families exchanging festive greetings over the airwaves increased her sense of isolation.

She had always loved Christmas. Now it felt hollow. She and Damien had been together but barely speaking the year before. She had a video of Jack opening presents. Since they separated, watching images of them with their child, filmed in the cold atmosphere of a disintegrating relationship, felt like a form of self-harm.

She had insisted she have the children for Christmas Eve. Why should Damien do so little and then get the best night of the year? She had made an effort to make it feel special for the children. Particularly Jack. They visited Santa's grotto, watched a Christmas film and left out carrots and milk when they went to bed. The hustle and bustle of the day had got her through. Now she was just feeling the raw pain of Christmas past, present and future.

She willed the children to wake up. As if on cue, Lizzy started crying from her room. Almost instantly, Jack ran in and threw himself on top of the king-sized duvet covering Sally. He was bouncing up and down with a huge smile across his face

"He's been! He's been! Can I open my presents Mummy? Please! Please?"

Sally was infected by his happiness. She grabbed Jack, put him on her lap and hugged him tightly.

"Of course, you can. But first I need to get Lizzy. She wants to be in here with us. She can open her presents too."

She held her cheeks against her small son's sweet-smelling skin, kissing the tip of his nose as she did so.

Jack pulled himself away. "Your face is wet!"

Lizzy was happy to be taken out of her cot and brought into the bedroom. Jack was on the carpet, already surrounded by piles of paper and toys. He gasped at each and every gift, then promptly put it down to open the next one.

Damien had agreed to the arrangement on condition the children went to him for their Christmas Dinner. Sally had felt she had no choice but to agree. The children would enjoy themselves. She could only fight one battle at a time. She did try to give Jack a sensible breakfast. It was inevitable he wanted to eat his entire selection box instead. She almost felt guilty when he moved onto the supersized Smarties pack. She didn't want Jack to be ill.

Sally dressed the children in smart new clothes. This year she had bought them two Christmas outfits each. She wanted them to look just as good at her parent's house on Boxing Day. It had meant spending yet more money she didn't have. Thank God for her credit card.

After more trips between the front door and the car boot than she cared to count, they were finally ready to leave. Sally seated herself behind the steering wheel and exhaled. She looked at the children in the rear view mirror. Jack screwed up his face. "I need a wee."

Lizzy could not be left alone in the car. Sally undid her car seat, lifted her out and took her into the living room. There was nowhere to put her down. Everything useful was packed. Sally went back outside with Lizzy still in her arms She instructed Jack to undo his seat belt and climb out by himself. She followed Jack back into the house. Jack got his step for the toilet and stood on it.

He flushed the chain, with a look of triumph on his face. "All done!"

Lizzy's nappy felt full. Sally retrieved the bag from the car's front seat and changed her quickly on the bathroom floor. Jack had found more Smarties. The chocolate was all over his fingers. Not yet on his new top. Sally left Lizzy on the floor, between her feet. She grabbed Jack and put his hands under the tap. Then she washed her hands and picked up Lizzy.

Sally put the children back in their car seats. She checked the front door was locked. Then she checked again. Finally, she got back in the car and drove off. Step one achieved.

***

This time, Sally had arranged to meet Jon at the new restaurant he had suggested. She was nervous. She had spent the last few days internally debating his intentions. She still had no idea if he really wanted to see her or whether he was he trying to be kind after she had thoroughly embarrassed herself.

She walked past the large windows populated by well-dressed diners at finely laid tables. She looked in. Jon was already there. He was standing in a small bar area, drinking the dregs of a pint of beer and looking towards the entrance.

Was she late? Too much or the right amount? Was there a right amount? She took a deep breath. She readjusted her skirt. Why had she let Lizzy persuade her to wear something so tight? It was too late now.

Jon's obvious pleasure at her arrival relaxed her. He gave her a peck on the cheek

"Drink?" he asked, putting his empty glass on the bar.

"Diet Coke please."

"Really?"

"I'm not going to drink tonight. Thought I'd stay sober."

"Is there a halfway house?"

Where had this man been hiding all her life? "Just one bottle then. To share."

After being settled at their tables, they ordered a starter and a main. Sally was taking no chances with an empty stomach this time. Her clinging skirt might make her regret the decision later. That would be the lesser of the two evils.

Jon poured them both a glass of the chilled House Chardonnay.

"How are Lizzy and Jack?"

"Oh, they're fine. Thanks. At least they were when I left them this evening. They're on their own tonight. I'm just praying they don't kill each other. Or set the house on fire."

"That's a low bar."

"You don't know them."

"Can't their dad help?"

"It's not worth asking. What about you? Is Beth with her mum?"

"Mandy is on a three-week women's retreat. She only sees Beth for a couple of hours every weekend anyway. She says she needs to find the woman inside her before she can find the mother."

Sally struggled to keep her views to herself. "And what do you think about that?" The golden rule of when in doubt, ask a question, had often proved useful.

"I think it's a load of bollocks."

She sat on her hands to prevent an instinctive celebratory punch in the air. If Jon had in any way entertained this nonsense from his ex, Sally would have had to put him right. She would have felt it her duty. But her outspokenness had got her into trouble before.

And Jon had almost sworn. She had begun to think he might have no faults at all. Not even small ones she quite liked. Such as saying 'bollocks' a bit too loudly in a posh restaurant.

"How do you juggle your job with looking after Beth?"

"I've gone part time. And Beth goes to one of her friend's houses before and after school. My mum helps out too."

Sally was asking too many questions. But she just couldn't stop herself. Jon had interviewed her already. It was time to turn the tables.

"What about your friends? Do you get out much?"

"Most of my friends were through Mandy. I didn't realise until she left. I've tried to be friendly with the school mums. Unfortunately, they either seem to be scared to talk to me because I'm on the telly or they drown me with sympathy because I'm a man."

"The 'poor you' brigade?"

"Yes. I don't mean to be ungrateful. But they seem to think I'm incapable. Single mums are just expected to get on with it. Single dads are congratulated for getting up in the morning. It makes me feel patronised, not proud. And it means we're not allowed into the 'gang'. Not really. Unless we're someone's pet project."

Sally had not heard a man say this before. She wasn't sure whether to cheer or give him a hug. She theatrically put her hand on his and squeezed it.

"Poor you."

Jon smiled. His eyes reflected the light from the candle on the table.

"I asked for that, didn't I?"

Neither of them moved their hands. Not until the waitress brought the soup.

***

The Christmas Present...

Damien's new home in the suburbs was on the way to her parents' house. He and Sharon had moved in shortly after making their relationship public. It had not felt right to stop the children going there. They hadn't stayed overnight yet but they had their own bedrooms and toys.

Sally pulled up outside. She took a moment to brace herself for what was to come.

"What are we waiting for Mummy? Are Daddy and Sharon not there?"

"They're inside. They're very excited about having you for Christmas Day."

Sally had decided from the start that she would not criticise Damien in front of the children. It wasn't easy. Today it felt particularly hard.

She released Jack from his car seat, placed him on the pavement and allowed him to run to Damien's front door. He could just about reach the doorbell when he stood on his toes. With Lizzy holding tight around her neck, her weight on her hip, Sally too made her way down the path.

Damien opened the door and picked Jack up. The father and son image reminded Sally of the 'perfect families' in old-fashioned mail order catalogues. When she had seen those pictures as a child she had not imagined the other woman moving into shot and possessively putting her hand on the father's shoulder.

It was Sharon who spoke first. "Hello Sally. Happy Christmas. Sorry I can't stop to talk. I'm cooking dinner for Ed and my parents."

Damien's dad playing happy families with Sharon felt like yet another betrayal.

"Is Ed here?" She peered into the hallway. It looked fantastic. Sharon had obviously spent a lot of time and effort making it festive. Sally and Damien had always favoured tacky and fun. These decorations were stylish and coordinated.

"Not yet. He won't be here for another hour or so."

Sally gave a sigh of relief. She did not want to have to make small talk with her soon to be ex father-in-law. Not in front of the person taking her place in so many ways.

Sharon did not appear to notice. "Anyway, busy, busy, have to love you and leave you. A woman's work is never done, as they say."

It took every ounce of Sally's willpower not to shout and scream at the woman who had more than doubled her own workload overnight.

She hurriedly handed Lizzy and her accompanying paraphernalia over to Damien, kissed the children goodbye, walked to the car, turned on the ignition, pulled out of the drive and clipped a red people carrier parked on the other side of the road.

Sally got out and surveyed the damage. She had knocked off her wing mirror. It was lying on the tarmac, the glass smashed. There was a small dent and big scratch in the other vehicle's passenger door.

"I'm so sorry!" she said to the woman who was coming out of the house opposite.

Two teenage children followed behind. Their Santa hats failing to mask their amazement at what they had just witnessed.

It was clear from her body language that the woman was losing her Christmas spirit.

"How did you manage...?"

"I'm really sorry. I've just dropped my children off at their dad's. I thought I could do it but it was just so hard. It's our first Christmas apart and..."

The woman put her hand on Sally's arm and gave her a comforting squeeze. Her demeanour had changed. Hostility had been replaced with kindness and compassion.

"Don't worry she said. It's just a car. I'm taking my children to their dad's too. I've been doing it for years. It really does get easier."

The young people behind her nodded in agreement.

***

Sally was disappointed when the coffees came. The bill would follow and then they would go their separate ways. She had really enjoyed the evening.

She could sense that Jon had too. She had not been looked at in that way for a very long time.

They paid for their meal and started making their way out of the restaurant. Jon stopped just as they got to the door. He leaned forward so their bodies were almost touching.

"Can I walk you home?" He lingered on the question.

"Yes."

His face was very close to hers. She wanted to kiss him. She didn't dare make the first move.

A crowd of people walked in noisily. Their chaotic entry forcing Jon and Sally apart and out of the door. They walked for several minutes in a charged silence.

Jon put his arm around Sally's waist. She liked it there. She felt good. She had not felt this good for a very long time. She also sensed something else. Something she had forgotten about entirely. It was as if a switch had been turned back on. An electric current was coursing through her veins. She imagined kissing Jon. Feeling his lips on her own.

She didn't want the evening to end. They were close to her house. Was she going to invite him in? Yes. No. Yes... Maybe. The children would be there of course. What would they make of her bringing a man home? They had never seen her do that before. But they had already met Jon. He wasn't a stranger. What if she asked him and he said no?

They approached her driveway. All the lights were on inside the house. How many times did she have to tell the children to switch them off when they went to bed? They would surely be in their rooms by now, if not actually asleep. She felt a ripple of irritation. She pushed it away. Nothing was going to spoil this moment.

They were at the front door. In the gloom of the porch, Sally fumbled in her bag for her keys. She found them. She pretended she was still searching. She needed more time.

Jon gently put his hand on her face. He tipped her chin towards him. Was this it? She moved closer. Their lips touched. Jon's were gentle and soft.

Suddenly they were showered with light. The front door opened wide. Damien stood silhouetted within its solid oak frame.

Christmas Selection Box

Your shopping list:
1. One Christmas Selection Box (available from all good supermarkets, September to December)

How to make it:
1. Open the box

Serve instead of breakfast on Christmas morning.

Chapter Six

"Damien! what are you doing here? Are the kids ok?"

Her ex-husband stood in the hallway. His shirt was untucked. He was in his socks. A toe was poking out of one of them. It was as if she was at the wrong house. Damien seemed so at home in this one.

"The kids are fine. They're in bed. They let me in. They said you wouldn't mind. Sharon's chucked me out. I need somewhere to stay."

"Since when did Jack and Lizzy make the decisions around here? You can't just turn up like this and make yourself at home! I've got company, you'll have to stay somewhere else."

"What company?"

Sally turned around to discover Jon had disappeared into the darkness.

She was very tired. She didn't have the energy to argue tonight. She stepped silently through the door and turned to go up the stairs. The children were standing at the top, in their pyjamas, watching their parents.

"You have to let him stay." Jack sounded determined. Lizzy nodded in a rare show of solidarity.

Sally looked back at their father. He had adopted the face that had once worked so well when he had wanted her to change her mind about something. It was surprising either of them could remember what it looked like.

Damien had won already.

"One night. That's all. I promise," he said, winking at the children.

She climbed the stairs, squeezed past her two betrayers, walked into her bedroom and closed the door.

She woke up in the morning still angry. With herself as much as Damien. Why had she not made him leave? Where was the strong woman she believed herself to be? Surely, he didn't still have some hold over her after all these years? Of course not! She had chosen to let him stay for sake of the children. Anyone would have done the same.

She could hear them all now, chatting cheerfully, directly below her room. The smell of bacon and eggs wafted up the stairs. It could almost have been a perfect family scene. The man she took pride in successfully living without, had his feet firmly under her kitchen table. Delighting their children with the culinary skills she was so lacking. She turned her body, put her face into her pillow and mouthed a silent scream.

She really liked Jon. She had hoped it might lead somewhere. That maybe he would be the storm to end her romantic drought. Instead, he had seen her throw up and be surprised by her ex-husband on her own doorstep. Two disastrous dates with the same man. That must be some kind of personal best.

There was a loud knock that was followed by Lizzy walking straight into Sally's room.

"Dad's making us breakfast. He says to ask if you want any. It's eggs and bacon. He bought them this morning. And he's found some frozen sausages. Can he cook them, please?"

"Has he told you when he's leaving?"

"He's got nowhere else to go. He would be on the streets. It's just for a while. He can sleep on the sofa bed."

Sally realised Damien had been cooking up more than breakfast that morning. "Tell him I'm not hungry."

Half an hour later, Sally made her way downstairs. She hesitated and looked through the doorway before entering the kitchen. Jack was at the table with his sister. It was an unusual sight. He normally sat at his computer from dawn till dusk. Longer, actually.

Damien was at the sink washing up. He turned to greet her.

"Morning! You look good."

Damien never complimented her. And she did not look good. She had showered and dressed but had not bothered to put any make up on or dry her hair.

"I know you said you didn't want anything. I've done you some tea and toast. And Jack's been back to the shop for orange juice."

It was as if she had stepped into an episode of Dallas. The one where Bobby Ewing came back from the dead and everyone pretended the last ten years hadn't happened.

She was not going to join in this charade.

"You can't stay here," she said.

Jack scowled.

Lizzy pouted.

Damien kept smiling.

"It's only for a bit," he said, in his gentlest voice. He seemed to have brought his whole toolbox from happier times.

"I promise not to get in your way. Sorry about that bloke last night. Wasn't he the one who interviewed you on the news?"

****

The application…

Sally was at her wits end. What should she do? She needed to be at work. She couldn't be late again this week.

The childminder had not turned up. And she had not answered her phone. That was what came of recruiting young girls straight out of college clutching their Level 3 BTEC Certificates in Childcare. For the very reason she employed them, she had no Plan B when they didn't show.

Panicked, she called Damien. When he answered, after several rings, his tone was not promising.

"What's the matter?"

"Emma's not turned up. I can ask Josie to take Jack to nursery. But there's no one to have Lizzy."

"You know it's 7am."

"Yes, Damien, I'm well aware of that. I was supposed to have left by now."

"Well I can't do it. What about your parents?"

"They've got work."

"Well, me too. I can't just take a day off when I fancy it."

Experience told her it was not worth pursuing the conversation. Not for the first time, she marvelled at how Damien had so easily made the mental leap from being a full-time dad to one who dipped in and out of parenthood when it suited him. She ended the call abruptly.

It was at times like this that she would reflect on the unfairness of it all. She and Damien had made a joint decision to get married, a joint decision to have children. Yet once he had made his unilateral decision to leave, she had been forced to become the default parent. He might look after them sometimes. Even buy them things when the mood took him. But his parenting was all at his discretion and within his control.

Sally had all the responsibility. It was assumed by Damien that she would have the children and give them what they needed. Always. As a matter of course. He was one step removed. For him, parenting was an optional pass time to be pursued at his convenience.

And what made it worse was that somehow that gave him added value. His actions were to be commented on and applauded. Worthy of note. Hers, on the other hand, were taken for granted. They were just what would be expected of any decent mother. She was the solid main meal. He was the side you wanted but didn't really need.

To be fair, her friends and family would often tell her what a great job she was doing. How Damien was shirking his duties. But even they slipped up occasionally. Her very supportive mum would sometimes say how good Damien was to have stayed on the scene. Why was that in any way remarkable?

Sally should not try to apply logic to these things. That way madness lay. If you sought clarity in confusion, rational thought in lies and excuses, you were doomed.

She breathed slowly in. Then out. A magazine article she'd read somewhere had said it was a good technique for staying calm and focussed. An idea came into her mind. Desperate times called for desperate measures.

Josie answered the door in her dressing gown, bleary eyed from being woken up just five minutes before by her anxious phone call. Good friends required little conversation. Sally bundled Jack through the door and hurried back into her own house. She grabbed her cargo and drove to her destination.

She walked into her newspaper's reception area on the local town's high street, both arms full and struggling under the weight. The receptionist continued talking on the phone, looked up, did a double take and said nothing. Sally walked past her, through a narrow door and into a tiny windowless room. The other half of the office's two person reporting team was already at his desk. He was smoking a cigarette. He quickly stubbed it out when he saw her come in.

"Isn't she a bit young for bring your daughter to work day?"

Sally opened up her portable play pen, with one hand and a few well-placed kicks, and put Lizzy inside.

"I've got nowhere else to take her, Tom." She waved her arms around to dissipate the smoke that had gathered in the room. This was starting to feel less and less like a good idea. She walked to the back of the office and opened the outside door.

"It won't be all day. I'll think of something. You won't tell, will you?"

"Of course not. But don't expect me to entertain her. I don't do babies."

"It's a deal."

She ran back to the car and returned with some toys. She put them beside Lizzy. Hopefully, they would keep her occupied until she actually did have a better idea.

Her colleague was watching everything, clearly bemused.

"Is this the modern face of parenting?"

"It's the modern face of single parenting."

Tom picked up another cigarette and his lighter and then put them down again, unused.

"You single mums. You want everything nowadays. Either you sit at home living off our taxes or you start demanding jobs with decent childcare. What was wrong with the workhouse?"

He didn't mean a word of it. He was one of the most decent men she had ever met.

Her editor called just as she sat down at her desk, demanding stories he could take to the morning briefing. He was obviously not impressed with her meagre offering of too frequent cancellations at a popular doctor's surgery. She agreed to ring a local councillor about plans for a new shopping centre. He was always ready with a controversial view. Perhaps she could ask him about subsidised nursery places at the same time.

She put the phone down and rested her head in her hands. Almost immediately, the room was again filled with the sound of urgent ringing. She looked around. Tom was quick to pick up calls. He must have already left on a story.

It was the head of communications at the local hospital. They had got to know each other well when local residents successfully fought plans to close the A&E. Sally heard herself being asked how she was. She answered on automatic pilot.

"Fine, thanks. How are you?"

Then, without any warning, she went into manual overdrive. Sally stopped pretending and let it all come out. The stresses and the strains of long working days, always being on call, evening shifts when she should be with her children. Finally, she finished, her words exhausted. Had she said too much?

"You need to change jobs."

"I know, I know. But it's not that easy. What would I do?"

"I need a media officer. You should apply."

****

Sally needed to not be in the house. Her house, that no longer felt like her own. She needed a friend.

103

As always, she went to Josie's back door, knocked loudly and opened it immediately.

"Hello!" She shouted

Josie's son, Andrew, was sitting at the kitchen table with his back to Sally. Dressed only in a pair of Hawaiian print boxer shorts, he appeared to be eating cereal with one hand while texting with the other.

"Oh! Sorry Andrew. I was sure your mum said you were going back to uni on Thursday."

Andrew muttered something indecipherable. He had been ten when Sally moved next door and became friends with his mother. He was not fazed by her sudden appearance. It was as though she was just another member of the family. He still hadn't looked up from his phone.

"Is your mum in?"

Finally, he tore himself away, just long enough to acknowledge her presence. "She's upstairs getting dressed."

He texted some more. He paused. Then he spoke as if the thought had only just occurred to him.

"Do you want me to get her?"

Sally shook her head and started to back out of the door she had just come through. Maybe she had called at a bad time.

"Hello! Sally! Where are you going? Andrew why didn't you tell me Sally was here? Honestly! And go and get dressed! Please! So, missus, tea? toast?"

"And bring that bowl back down when you've finished with it!" Josie shouted after Andrew as he walked out of the room with his phone and his breakfast.

It was at times like these that Sally realised why Josie's friendship meant so much to her. One hour, two cups of tea and two slices of toast later, she had recounted the last twelve hours. Josie had little patience with Damien and his track record as a father. His role in the story had clearly done nothing to change that.

"What are you going to do about your squatter? You don't want him to stay do you?"

"Of course not. But I can't let the kids see me kick him out. I don't know why he's here. And he's being so nice."

"That's when you need to worry. Nice never ends in anything good. He's charming you because he wants some free accommodation for a while. What's he done that's upset Sharon so much?"

"I don't know and I don't care."

"Well give him a deadline to leave, tell the kids and stick to it. You need to take control, Sally, of everything."

Josie was right, of course. Sally wanted to change the conversation.

"Like you have, you mean."

Josie took a deep breath.

"It's a long story," she said. "One I should have told you years ago."

"Well tell me now."

Josie got up to put the kettle on for the third time.

"At first I thought I was a failure. Why couldn't I make my marriage work when others could? I just wanted to curl up in a ball and hide from the world. Money troubles meant I had to go out. I needed to make a living. But I didn't feel worthy of anything else."

Josie busied herself with making the coffee. It was clear her flow of consciousness should not be interrupted.

"The 'milk man incident' changed everything. I saw that I was still the same person inside that I had always been. But I had grown stronger. I wasn't ashamed. I was proud. I didn't want or need a partner. Certainly not another husband. Why should that mean I never have sex again? I've always enjoyed it. I wasn't going to let divorce take that away from me too.

"When we were married, the boys' dad brought home the money and I ran the house. When he left, and the money dried up to nearly nothing, I didn't sit at home with the boys and let us starve. I went out and got a job. Well what's the difference with sex really? As long as everyone understands the arrangement, we all win."

Josie placed the coffee on the table and sat down. The two women sat in a loud silence, for a few minutes, broken by the sound of Josie opening a packet of chocolate biscuits.

"After a while I found it was easier to stick to men in uniform."

"Soldiers and sailors!"

"In Birmingham? I don't think so! More rat catchers and removals. They know how to get things done. And how to keep things quiet."

"How have you managed to keep this quiet from me for so long? Hang on, I remember when I had a rat catcher. Jack…"

"You moved house, too. I have more to thank you for than you know."

Josie was on a roll.

"Our eyes met over a tub of rat poison. Or boxed up possessions. My own version of Mills and Boon. Why would I refuse them?"

"Them?!"

"Calm down. I only do these things one at a time. The rat catcher came to my house after yours. He was particularly attractive. I wasn't even trying that time. He made it obvious he liked me. I didn't know it then but we Hexagons can recognise each other."

"Hexagons?"

"House sEX And GONe. Do you like it? I made it up. There's loads of us. Hiding in plain sight."

Had Sally been sleepwalking all these years? Who was this woman sitting opposite? And why did Sally admire her even more than she had before?

Josie put the refilled mugs of coffee on the table and put a biscuit in her mouth. She didn't let that stop her story.

"He clearly understood I was shopping. He made it obvious his services were for hire. And I don't mean his rat catching skills. He offered to come back after he had finished his shift. To help me clear the rubbish out of my garage that the rats had seemed to love so much."

"And did he?"

"Well he came. But not in the garage."

***

The work experience…

Lizzy was content in her workplace play pen for the first hour. She had always been easy. Just like a handbag, you needed to know she was safe but she demanded little attention. It meant there was time for a call to the doctors' surgery and the rent-a-quote councillor and for some copy to be filed.

It was not Sally's best work. Neither story would be positioned more prominently than page nine. But at least she had a made a contribution to that day's paper. And her hospital contact had given her an exclusive for tomorrow. That should please her editor. Possibly for the first time in weeks.

She might actually get away with smuggling her daughter into the office. She had made some other phone calls too. She only needed to juggle things for two more hours. Then her mum could come and pick Lizzy up.

She was more relaxed than she had been at any other point that morning. She watched her little girl play with her favourite toys. Rabbit and Doll had arrived and been christened shortly after Damien left. Sally had named them. She had not felt very creative. The phone rang again. Lizzy turned Rabbit towards the noise and pointed. She seemed to know it had to be answered.

Sally calmly picked up the handset. She put it down in a panic. A young woman had died in a freak cycling accident on a country lane. Her editor wanted her to get an interview with the family. Preferably a picture. At the very least a quote.

Sally hated these stories. She felt as if she was preying on people's grief. Even if they did sometimes want to talk about their loved one. And others certainly wanted to read about them. Yet she seemed to be good at them. In the midst of their anguish, families would open up and talk to her. It was a mixed blessing. It made each one a little bit easier. It also meant she was asked to do them more often.

But it wasn't the task itself that was worrying her today. It would have been risky to take Lizzy with her on any story. It was out of the question on this one. How could she leave Lizzy behind? How could she refuse to go out on a story without saying why? Lizzy stood up in her play pen and stretched out her arms, as if hearing her mother's thoughts.

Sally picked her up and stood there for a moment. Should she say she felt ill and just go home? She wished she'd done that in the first place. She had not wanted to give those who assumed she would struggle as a single working parent any more ammunition than they already had.

At this moment the receptionist walked into the back room. This time she smiled fondly at Lizzy and gave Sally a sympathetic look.

"There's two sixth formers from the local comp at the desk. Do you or Tom know anything about them? They're not in my diary. They might be the answer to your prayers."

Sally did not believe in God but perhaps there was a single parent fairy. She thanked both of them under her breath just in case and went out to the reception area.

"Hello girls, how do you fancy a different kind of work experience?"

***

Sally was making tea. Damien had offered but she had told him she was perfectly capable, thank you. He had already cooked the previous two nights while she took a bath. He was making himself far too useful.

She climbed on a chair to reach the ready prepared kit of jars and pasta sheets from the top shelf of the cupboard. She sensed the children were sharing an in joke with their dad when she got down and placed the pack on the kitchen table.

She checked the fridge for mince and cheese. Good. She didn't a need mad rush to the shops. She turned the dial on the oven to the right temperature and pressed the button marked 'OK'. She checked the oven light had come on. She browned the mince and added the jar of tomato sauce. She wondered if she should call Jon.

She spread some of the meat sauce onto the bottom of a baking dish she had fished out of the saucepan drawer. It had been three days since they had got back to the house and Damien had interrupted them on the porch. And she had not heard from Jon since.

She laid the pasta sheets on top of the meat sauce and spooned some of the jar of white sauce onto the pasta. Should she have sent him a message the next morning? Apologised? Explained?

She repeated the process until she had run out of mince then topped it off with more pasta and white sauce. She had not known what to say. She still had no idea.

She grated some cheese, scattered it on top of the white sauce and put the lasagne in the oven. Why was Jon staying silent?

He knew where she lived. He had all her numbers. Beyond the obvious, it was hard to think of a good reason why he had not been in touch. Her teenage self might have optimistically imagined he had been hit by a steam train and was lying in a hospital somewhere, injured, unable to reach a phone. Or that perhaps he had been kidnapped by a magic circle cult.

But she had categorical proof he was fine. He had appeared on last night's Look Midlands, fit as a fiddle.

She put the television on now. There he was again. He was attempting a Paso Doble. At least that's what she thought he said. He seemed to be enjoying himself.

"I think I've managed to prove that to come dancing with the award winning Second City Dance Academy is strictly something for the professionals," he said into the camera.

Sally did not like where his dance partner was putting her hands. Not. At. All.

***

The knock…

Twenty minutes after persuading the students and receptionist that Lizzy would be fine for the hour she'd be gone, Sally was pulling up outside the house where the now dead girl had lived with her parents.

She had not had time to worry about what she would say to the mum and dad whose lives had been broken and scattered earlier that morning.

Death knock. That was how it was known in the trade. Sally considered the term as she walked up the garden path. Horrible. Appropriate. They die. We knock.

Or press. She raised her hand to ring the bell. The door opened before she had chance to do so. A red-haired woman too young to be the mother of a teenager stood facing her. Her hair was unbrushed and her face was covered in the raw streaks of unending tears. Sally did not see her take aim. She did feel the sharp sting of a hand meeting her cheek.

"Go away. They've already talked to you. You lot are all scum. My sister's died and you're here pestering my mum and dad. They might be too nice to get rid of you but I'm not."

The slap shocked Sally into silence. She turned and walked quickly back to her car. The young woman followed her, shouting angrily. Sally jumped in and locked the doors. She could see the woman in her rear view mirror, peering in.

Her assailant appeared to spot Lizzy's car seat and blanket in the back of the car. Sally saw the look of pure hate that had been there for the last few minutes fade away. Then she saw the head of red hair turn away from her and move back towards the house.

What was left of Sally's composure disintegrated. Yet again she found herself crying in the front seat of her Ford Focus. It had become her private space to rail against the world.

She felt only shame at what she had driven that woman to do. She had no time to seek out good stories. She was too tired to write them when they fell in her lap. She had left Lizzy in the arms of strangers. She did not feel like a good person, a good journalist or even a good mum

Her life was different now. She would apply for the job at the hospital. Make a change. But this did not alter the here and now. If she told her editor she had been sent packing, there would be no sympathy for her or the bereaved family. Just a demand to get back out there and try again. And again. Until they gave in and she had her story. She was not going back to that front door. Nor anyone else's, in similar circumstances. Ever.

She jumped at three short sharp raps on the car window. Was her pursuer back? She should have driven away as soon as she had the chance. Fearfully she turned her head towards the sound. Her face was still smarting from the smack she had received just minutes before. She could see only a blue tie on a smart, white, shirt, tucked into black slim-waisted trousers.

The man wearing the clothes bent down so she could see his face. With a disarming smile, he indicated for her to wind the window down. She had never seen this tall, rather handsome person before. He looked harmless. But she was still wary. She lowered the window just enough to hear what he was saying.

"Hi. Are you ok? I saw what happened. I'd only just finished talking to them. The sister arrived as we were packing up. I think they hoped we would be the last."

He flashed his BBC pass at her as he spoke.

She lowered the window a bit further.

"Who do you work for? If it's a paper, I'm happy to give you something you can use."

"Second City Post. That would be fantastic. Thank you."

This dark-haired stranger had unexpectedly turned out to be Sally's saviour. She could go back to the office with something to show for her efforts. Sally lowered the window all the way.

The man scribbled left handed into his notepad. He shook his pen. Then tried again. Without thinking, Sally handed him the silver fountain pen her mum had bought her for her twenty-first birthday. She used it every day at work. It was her professional lucky charm. Although it hadn't brought her much luck today.

He wrote something down, ripped out the page and passed it to Sally. His handwriting was terrible. Sally took a moment to decipher the note's contents.

Marion was the light of our lives. The world is a darker place without her

She realised he had probably given her his best quote. She looked up again to thank him. He had gone from the window. He was crossing the road to his own car further ahead. A bald cameraman was waiting for him.

"Come on Jon," he said urgently. "They want us to film at the scene of the accident."

It was only much later that she realised she had lost her pen.

***

"Smells good. Do you want me to do a salad?"

Damien was standing too close. Invading more than just her kitchen. He picked up the remote and turned off the television. Without waiting for an answer, he started chopping up some peppers and washing lettuce. She didn't remember buying either of them. Was she supposed to be grateful?

Sally checked her mobile and her landline again for any missed calls. Nothing. The sound of something being pushed through the door interrupted her thoughts. She walked through to the hall. A letter was on her mat. She didn't think people wrote to each other anymore. It was almost exciting to see her name on an envelope. Although something about the bad handwriting told her it was not good news.

115

She ripped it open and unfolded the note inside. Her eyes went straight to the end.

Lasagne

Your shopping list:
1. One jar creamy lasagne sauce
2. One jar tomato-based lasagne sauce
3. Pasta sheets
4. 400g mince
5. 50g cheese

How to make it:
1. Brown the mince in a little oil. Once cooked, add the tomato-based sauce to the mince and stir through.
2. Coat the base of an ovenproof dish with a thin layer of the mince and lay three lasagne sheets on top.
3. Spread the creamy lasagne sauce on top of the sheets, then cover with more mince. Repeat the layers - pasta, creamy sauce and mince – until you have used all the mince.
4. Add a final layer of pasta, then top with the remaining creamy lasagne sauce and sprinkle with grated cheese.
5. Place the lasagne in a hot oven at 180^{0}C/Gas Mark 4 for 30mins.

Serve when golden brown with a side salad or veg.

Chapter Seven

The brood…

"That one mummy. He likes me."

"Careful Jack. Don't poke your fingers in. You might frighten him."

Sally liked that one too. he balls of brown fur were all so small and intertwined. It was hard to tell where one finished and another started. This one had distinguished itself by waking and revealing its bright green eyes. A decision had to be made. It was as good a way to decide as any.

Sally had told the children that morning that they were going to get a pet. They were as excited as she had hoped they would be. As a child, she'd grown up with animals. She wanted her children to have that pleasure too.

She had not been able to provide them with a two-parent home. She could and would give them those markers of positive family life that were in her gift.

Her preference was for a dog. To keep them company. To guard them at night. To blame for the strange noises as their semi-detached creaked and Sally froze under the bed covers.

But a dog was not practical. She was not in the house enough. When would she walk it? She was already struggling with all she had to do each day. She would have to banish her fears of burglars and bandits. She had coped with so much already. Just let them come! She would do anything required to fiercely protect her brood.

So here they were, choosing a kitten at the local rescue centre. She could not stop looking at his mother. Suckling her babies. Still so young herself. Already unwanted. Sally stroked the jet-black fur of this feline single mum.

"We need to stick together. Do you and your little one want to come home with us?"

***

Dear Sally,

I wanted to thank you for the two enjoyable evenings we spent together.

I can see that your life is very complicated right now. I think I should give you the space to do what is best for you and your family.

I need to think of my daughter too. I do not want to make things any more confusing for her than they already are.

I wish you well, now and always,
Jon xx

"Getting love letters already?"

Damien made her jump. He had to stop creeping up on her like this. She quickly folded up the letter and put it in the back pocket of her jeans. She tried to suppress the turmoil she was feeling. She could not let him see. She hadn't noticed she'd been holding her breath until she tried to speak.

"It's from Helen."

"Helen? I haven't seen her since Jack's third birthday party. She gave me such a dirty look when I came round the house. Put me right off her."

Sally decided not to dignify his remark with a response. If he was hoping to show he had changed he needed to try a lot harder. At least his attention had been diverted away from Jon's note.

"I didn't set out to hurt you," he said.

"Well you succeeded."

Sally regretted her instinctive come-back. She had long stopped engaging in any war of words with Damien. She wanted to get away. To lick her wounds. Not any inflicted by her former husband. Those had either healed or she'd stopped noticing them. It was a fresh cut that was hurting her now.

"It was a long time ago Damien. Let's not go back there."

"I know. I don't want to go back either. I'm not the same person I was then. I made mistakes. Let's start from now."

He looked her straight in the eyes. Sally accidentally met his gaze. It was the first time they had looked at each other directly since he had walked out on her in the play barn all those years before.

"I can help out with the meals," Damien continued. "And in other ways. I won't be a nuisance."

Sally stayed silent. SHE was not the same person either. And it wasn't just the last fifteen years that had changed her.

She felt different from the woman she was just a few weeks ago. Whatever had been sleeping inside her had stirred. She had allowed herself to get close to Jon. To believe she might once again be able to trust a man with her whole self. To have feelings that had excited and scared her in equal measure. She did not know what to do with her homeless emotions.

Damien poured her a glass of Merlot.

***

The ring…

Sally hoisted her daughter onto her other hip and opened the front door to the childminder. Lizzy was dressed in only a nappy. Jack was racing around the living room in Thomas the Tank Engine pants and T-shirt, pretending to be a train.

"Sorry I'm late," said Emma breezily, stepping into the house and taking Lizzy from Sally's arms.

Guilt pressed down on Sally's chest. Why was she trusting her children with someone who was often late and never truly sorry? Something caught Sally's eye. On Emma's right hand was a gold ring with a large ruby at its centre. Sally recognised it straight away. It was the one Damien put on her finger the day they got engaged.

"Why are you wearing my ring?"

Emma looked down. She flushed as red as the stone before quickly regaining her composure.

"I found it on the floor. I put it on to remind myself to give it to you. I must have forgotten."

"Yes. Sparkly gemstones can be easy to miss."

Sally grabbed her work bag and rushed out the door. As she put the key in her car's ignition she stopped still. What was she doing? Nothing was more important than her children. Not her career, not her pride.

When Damien left, she had worn her wedding and engagement rings for a few more months. She wasn't ready for the difficult conversations their absence might trigger. Then, after coming home to find Sharon hiding behind her living room door, she had removed them. Doing so had felt important and symbolic. She had placed them in a jewellery box inherited from her grandmother. She had put the box at the back of her dressing table drawer. They had been out of the reach of her children. But not out of the grasp of a prying childminder.

She was gripping the steering wheel so hard her knuckles hurt. She lifted her head high and went back into the house. Emma was in the kitchen making herself a cup of coffee.

Lizzy was wearing a dress that looked as if it had been pulled from the top of the dirty washing basket. Jack was still a semi naked locomotive. Emma had taken the ring off her finger and placed it on the worktop.

"You're sacked." The words felt good.

Emma stuttered something incomprehensible. Without another word she left the way she had come in just minutes before.

Sally rang work complaining of a terrible headache. She wasn't going to attempt anything else today, whatever people thought. Well, just one thing. Three hours later, she bundled the children into the car and made a quick trip to the newsagent's for her paper's first edition.

Back home she flattened the newspaper out on the table in front of her. She had been promised the job was going to be advertised that morning. And there it was.

Within the pages of the very thing she needed to escape from. The key to her freedom. A nine to five job. Working as a press officer for a hospital. She could find a childminder she could rely on. She could know her children were in good hands. She rang the number and asked for an application form. It felt like a new beginning.

***

Sally walked through the unassuming back entrance of her city centre office building. When visitors entered from the front they could tell it used to be a bank. The grand columns, high ceilings and sculptured cornices gave the game away. In stark contrast, the staff entrance boasted a small security desk, old carpet and uncollected parcels. It's one advantage was that it was nearer to the station.

She had got to know most of the security team after so many years of walking past them three times a day. Morning, noon and night. She had tried to work out in her head how many times she must have said hello and waved her pass at whoever was behind the counter. She had concluded it was a lot.

Adam was her favourite. Tall, broad shouldered and round. He was what she would have called a gentle giant in her newspaper days. As was often the case with security men, for reasons not clear to Sally, he was bald. Just a small, goatie beard told the world that he once probably had a mop of ginger hair. Nearing retirement, he was laid back and cheerful. Counting the days until he could be relaxing full-time in the garden with his wife and grandchildren.

"Hello Sally. You're early today."

She checked the time. It was 8am. How had she managed to be there an hour earlier than usual?

She had got up the same time as always. Followed the same morning pattern of showering, dressing and doing her hair and make-up. All the while listening to Radio Four. Once it had been Radio One. Then Radio Two. She hadn't particularly noticed each time she had moved her listening up the dial but it had happened all the same.

It was when she came downstairs that things had changed. Damien had corralled the kids through breakfast and into the car. He had even cooked eggs and washed up. He had obviously been feeling very pleased with himself.

"I'll take them to school. I'll pick them up too. And I'll cook tea again. Let me know if you're going to be late and I'll put a plate in the oven for you. I decided sausage casserole. You've got the jar. I'll pick up the rest. We all like that don't we?"

Sally wasn't sure how he was going to fit his own job into this busy schedule. She didn't really care. He worked for Sharon's dad as the manager of his haulage firm. Perhaps he was trying to avoid his almost father-in-law.

"New routine," she replied to Adam. He looked up and smiled over the top of his newspaper.

Her office was located on the first floor. The remaining six levels were home to solicitors, government quangos and administrative teams for large companies. She knew none of them. She walked up the stairs, through yet more security doors and into the open-plan office.

Today she had the pick of the workstations. Just two of her colleagues were already seated. They looked surprised to see her joining them, in the work equivalent of the dawn chorus. She chose a spot in the hub of the office. Connected her laptop to the monitor. Signed herself into her phone.

"Hey! Have you finally sold the kids into slavery?"

It was Helen.

"Tempting." Sally countered. "Damien's staying."

"Damien's staying? I hope you haven't forgotten what that man did to you?"

"Of course not. He hasn't got anywhere else to go. He and Sharon have had a row."

"What about your new boyfriend? Who you still haven't told me about by the way. Your life is becoming like a soap opera. I won't need to bother with Eastenders soon."

"You've never bothered with Eastenders. Thanks for the kind words though."

"Anytime. In return for my supportive friendship, I was hoping you could come with me for my scan next week."

Sally was glad to have a big announcement at work to prepare for that day. They were launching an important strategy. Focussing on press releases and ministerial photo calls took her mind off missed opportunities.

She arrived home exhausted. Usually that was a recipe for disaster. Today, the house was calm, tea was cooking, everything was where it should be. This must be what a two-parent household felt like. A family.

Damien shattered the illusion.

"Sharon insists on cooking everything from scratch. She won't have these jars in the house."

Sally went to the fridge. "Is there a bottle open?"

Curled up in the settee with a glass in her hand, she ignored the television. She couldn't risk seeing Jon again. Not now. Music was a safer choice. Something from the eighties when life felt less complicated.

Someone else getting the children out of the house in the morning had meant she could calmly get ready for work. Someone home in time to cook the tea every day would remove the pressure she began to feel at four pm.

She could be one of those people who were able to stop and chat. Or go for a drink after work. And if the children wanted to talk, she would be relaxed enough to really take in what they were saying. The stresses and strains of the last few years were lifting from her shoulders.

"Where's the remote."

She was surprised to find she had been asleep. "Your dad tidied up, Jack. Ask him."

"He's gone out."

"Where?"

"I don't know. He didn't say."

"Have you looked in the drawer under the telly. The one for the remote?"

The television sprang to life. Sally stood up. She needed to change out of her work clothes. Tea would be ready soon. It was odd that Damien had chosen now to pop out. Well, she wasn't his keeper. And thankfully the sausage casserole wasn't her problem.

In her bedroom now, she put on her scruffy jeans and T-shirt, then picked up a magazine and started to read. She heard Damien return and call them all to the table. She was in danger of getting used to this.

After they'd eaten, Jack, Lizzy and Damien squeezed onto the sofa together, playfully arguing about what to watch. Damien won. It was a programme about cars. It was churlish not to join them.

Two hours later they were all still there. They were binge watching a series of half hour repeats on returning classic vehicles to their former glory. Sally was drinking the bottle of wine on the coffee table in front of her. Her mobile started buzzing, making her glass and its contents vibrate. Damien picked the phone up and passed it to her. Was it her imagination or did a shadow of disapproval fleetingly cross his face?

She slid her finger across the screen and put it to her ear. "Hello?"

"Hi, it's that bossy woman who lives next door. You might remember me."

Sally immediately felt guilty. She had neglected Josie.

Damien flashed her a sideways look. There was no question this time.

She moved out into the hall.

"Sorry I haven't been round lately. It's..." Sally started.

"I know what it is. You've been kidnapped by that ex-husband of yours. Now you've got Stockholm Syndrome and you're starting to like your captor."

Sally was glad the call was out of Damien's hearing.

"It's not like that." Sally heard her voice inflect upwards. As though she was asking a question rather than making a statement.

"Well, Rachel and I are preparing a raid. You're coming out with us Saturday night whether you like it or not. And put on your glad rags. Gaining your freedom is the first objective. Losing your celibacy record with someone other than your ex-husband is the second."

"Damien? Josie! Absolutely not!"

"It's non-negotiable," Josie continued. "We need to move fast so I'm taking matters into my own hands. Rachel needs a night out too. Those twins are a handful. Even with two and a half adults in the house."

Putting up a fight would be futile.

Josie did not wait around for one.

"See you at mine. Seven pm for 'pre-drinks' as the young people like to say. And don't be late. If I sense any wavering, I shall come and get you. Now go and shave your legs! And you might want to think about other parts of your anatomy too."

Josie ended the call. Sally paused before returning to the living room. They had moved on to episode six.

***

The numbers…

Sally looked at the numbers scribbled across two sheets of A4 paper. As if staring at them for long enough would make them add up. It wasn't working. However hard she tried. She could not make the money coming in exceed what was going out.

She was one of the lucky ones. She had won in the lottery of life that had given her the health and intelligence needed to secure and hold down a job that paid well and had prospects. But she had lost in the lottery of love. Running a household single handed meant carrying the weight of more responsibility than she sometimes believed she could manage.

She looked again at her accounts book where she meticulously wrote down every financial transaction. Lots going out. Little coming in.

OUT: The bills. Fewer adults in the house did not mean fewer demands. The mortgage. Borrowed based on two salaries, now paid by one. The childcare. The more she worked, the more she paid. Historical Loans. Foolishly taken out with Damien. The unexpected costs of growing infants. It would only get worse when they started school.

IN: Her salary. Child benefits. Maintenance.

Damien paid a set-price for child raising. He knew exactly how much his children were going to cost him. No nasty surprises ever came his way. He didn't seem to understand that the expense of children didn't conform to monthly standing orders. When he paid in full, it barely covered his share of their old debts, never mind that month's expenses. Yet he couldn't even stick to that. Cash gifts from her brother who worked abroad were a godsend.

It could be worse. She was very grateful it wasn't. She still could not make money she didn't have stretch to the end of the month. Not for the first time, Sally wondered what on her 'out' list she could lose or ignore. Everything felt essential. She could re-sole her shoes again rather than get a new pair. That barely touched the problem. She could try not to use her car too often. That was tricky.

Sally wanted to work. She could sell the house, move in with her parents and claim benefits. She didn't blame others for making that choice. But for her, it was just not an option she wanted to take. She was not prepared to let Damien rob her of the career opportunities she had worked so hard to win.

She wanted her children to have their own home, holidays and treats. She wanted to give them the kind of childhood she had enjoyed. She wanted them to have a successful, ambitious mother as their role model. She had created her own challenge. However unwise, it was a rod she could not bring herself to put down.

And why would her friends reduce the invitations to socialise when they had no clue that the lifestyle they saw did not reflect her bank balance? Why would she say no when their friendship was what got her through?

She would have to use a pay day loan again. She knew how bad they were. How shocked her colleagues family and friends would be if they found out. The secret shame was better than the public embarrassment of borrowing from them.

Damien and Sally had made an unaffordable bed. Now she, alone, was lying in it.

***

"What's your poison?" Josie was getting her purse out of her bag.

"Any cocktail. You choose for me," said Sally. "And let's have a kitty. Rachel should pay less as our designated driver."

"Good idea," said Josie. "£20 from me and you and a tenner from Rach should do us. At least for now! Sex on the beach Sally? We need to get you into practice for the real thing!"

They were in a new cocktail bar in the town's high street. At Josie's house they had consumed a bottle of wine and two glasses of lemonade between them. Sally was feeling pleasantly relaxed. Just enough not to be thrown by the exorbitant prices and being Josie's project for the night.

Was this the sort of place where people their age went to meet others for a night of passion with no names and no pack drills? Josie had implied as much. She looked around the opulently furnished bar. The men and women had all clearly made an effort. She had always found smartly dressed men attractive. She liked what she saw.

One of the men was looking in their direction. He was in the shadows, so she hadn't spotted him at first. Was he looking at her? It felt like he might be. That was fast. Could it be this easy? Not that she would be going through with anything.

He was staring. It was bordering on rude. Oh God. Was he walking over? Her view was blocked by Josie returning to their table with the round of drinks. Sally picked hers up and drank almost the whole glass. She felt the hit from the vodka. The man had now stepped into the better lit part of the bar. He was fast approaching them. He gave a friendly wave.

Josie had spotted him too. "He's a bit forward!"

Sally felt a shiver across her whole body. She tipped her glass and finished the last dregs. "He's George!"

Sausage Casserole

Your Shopping List

1. 500g jar Sausage Casserole sauce
2. 8 good quality sausages

How to make it

1. Preheat your oven (190°C/Gas Mark 5/Fan 170°C).
2. Fry sausages until evenly browned (about 10 minutes).
3. Place sausages into an ovenproof casserole dish (2L) and pour on your sauce.
4. Cover and cook in your oven for 35 minutes.

Ensure food is fully cooked and piping hot throughout before serving.

Leave to stand for 5 minutes.

Enjoy with mashed potato and your family.

Chapter Eight

"George? Who's George?" said Josie.

Sally tried to speak. She realised her mouth was already gaping open. She closed it quickly. Rachel got in first. "The one that got away."

George reached the table. Sally stared at his face. He looked the same to her as he had twenty years before. The day they said goodbye.

"Hello Sally," he said. "I thought it was you. Long-time no see."

Sally continued staring. His boyish charm and chiselled good looks were just as attractive to her now as they had been then. She was startled by a sharp elbow in the ribs. Josie was looking at her pointedly.

"Oh. Sorry. Hello George. What a surprise."

"A good one I hope," said George. He turned to a man Sally had not noticed until this moment. "This is Stephen. Can we buy you and your friends a drink?"

"You most certainly can," said Josie.

George turned and gave her what had to be his most engaging smile. Sally could see he was more practised at this than when she had last been in his company.

"Great. What are you having?" he said.

George smoothly took their orders and headed to the bar. The second man who had not yet said a word to anyone followed behind him.

"Gorgeous George!" said Josie. "You said he was a hunk! Remind me again why you let him go?"

"He wanted to be a sea captain. I didn't want to be a sea captain's wife," said Sally.

"How about a sea captain's bit on the side?" Josie got up from where she had been sitting next to Sally and deposited herself on the same side of the table as Rachel.

George returned with a tray full of drinks. He positioned himself by the now vacant chair.

"Do you ladies mind if we join you? After six months working together Stephen and I have pretty much run out of conversation."

Sally wondered if Stephen ever had any conversation. He reminded her of Simon, the Look Midlands cameraman. Then Simon reminded her of Jon. More than one man had got away.

George flashed his perfect white teeth at Josie again.

"We'd be delighted," she said.

****

The christening…

Sally couldn't quite believe it. Surely Damien hadn't meant it when he said he would not be coming to

Lizzy's christening. They had been rowing on the doorstep again. They had both said things they didn't mean. At least that was what she had assumed last night.

She had told him he was not pulling his weight. She had wanted a night away. He had refused to have the children. They were yet to sleep in the child friendly bedrooms he had created for them. She had called him names. He had told her to grow up. Then it had got really bad.

She didn't recognise the man he was now. His transformation reminded her of the film *Invasion of the Body Snatchers*. Despite his new 'trendy' clothes and hair style, he looked and sounded pretty much the same. People behaved as it if it was him. They were convinced it was him. But he wasn't the man she had married. Maybe she just had to accept he was a different person. Manage her expectations around this stranger.

Everyone was in the church. Everyone except Damien. They were due to start the service in five minutes. Sally looked across from where she was standing at the back. The beautiful old building was full of people. Happy families with their babies. Mums AND dads.

Lizzy was sitting on her grandad's lap looking beautiful. Jack was under the pews playing with his cars. Her mum was trying to keep him quiet. Rachel and Karl were there. So too, were Michael and Serena, with their own baby, born just weeks before. And Helen, looking fabulous in a dress that probably cost the same as Sally's monthly mortgage payment.

The vicar gestured to Sally that they were about to start. She walked to where the people she loved were sitting. Single parenthood might have been a baptism of fire, but she would not let herself or her children get burnt.

***

Sally was torn. Seeing George had made her heart beat fast and her pulse quicken. She was clearly still attracted to him. She wanted nothing more than to sit down and catch up. But not here, not now. Not with Josie and Rachel and some stranger watching. She could feel herself going red. It was not her best look.

The last time George had seen her, they had been in their early twenties. Time had not been as kind to her as it had to him. Childbirth had been pretty mean too. At least she'd made an effort with her appearance tonight. She would be eternally thankful she had not bumped into him in a supermarket, on a random Saturday. Wearing no make-up and in clothes splattered with that day's tea.

George sat down. Stephen followed. Josie and Rachel turned to him. It seemed he could speak after all. Soon all three were chatting and laughing. Engrossed in a conversation that involved Kate Winslet and whistles.

George looked directly at Sally. It was as if they were the only two people in the room. Just as when they had met all those years before, in the first few minutes of a marathon school disco. It would have been more honest if they had been sponsored for kissing rather than dancing. They had been by each other's side throughout the next 24 hours and then for the next five years.

They must have had silly teenage rows, although Sally couldn't remember any of them. They had been happy. They had enjoyed each other's company. Sex was uncomplicated and fun. What more could they ask for? It had probably never been quite that good again.

Sally had been convinced they would eventually get married, move to the countryside and have babies, whilst somehow both pursuing successful careers. She needed to go to university first of course, if she was going to be a successful journalist. Back then she believed she could have it all.

George had been less clear about his future. He was happy to take life as it came. Sally had realised much later that she had taken his ambivalence to her plans as consent. And that they were not the same thing.

He did have one passion. Ships. How they were constructed and how they worked. He studied the sea. Reading books in his landlocked Midlands home. When Sally set off for university, he was talking of little else. By the end of her first year he had taken a job as a trainee officer on a cruise ship.

"So how long's it been, Sally?" George asked. "You don't look any different!"

"Well you've changed," said Sally. "You definitely weren't such a smooth talker."

"Schmoozing is part of the job description for a Captain. Why do you think everyone wants to sit at our table?"

"Captain!" said Sally. The incredulity in her voice ringing louder than she had intended.

"Well thanks for the vote of confidence," said George. "I happen to think I'm a rather good Captain."

Sally was impressed. She didn't want George to know. Nor the effect he was having on her vital signs. Or was that the cocktails?

"Well, tonight you've sat at our table, so don't get too big for your boots."

"Not with you, Sally. How could I? I'm so pleased to see you. You really do look great."

Sally felt like she was 17 again, attending one of their friends' many 18th birthday parties together. All her sixth form classmates had been jealous. They couldn't quite understand why he had chosen her. It had all seemed so perfect. Why hadn't they tried harder to make it work?

After George took his job they had only been able to see each other for a few weeks every six months. There was no social media then of course. At first, they wrote every day. Then the letters started to dry up. When they were together, they knew less and less about the person each of them was becoming.

They were both stepping out into the big wide world. Maybe each believed the other might be holding them back from finding its true treasures. What if they HAD made that extra effort? Would they still be together now? Married? Children?

"Are you married? Children?" asked George.

"Divorced. And two. A boy and a girl. Teenagers"

"Snap!"

Sally might just crumple under her chair. She was cross with her younger self. The one who assumed everything was going to be so easy.

"Do you miss them, being away so much?" she asked.

"Who?"

"Your children."

"Oh right, sorry! Think I may have just answered your question! Yes, of course I do. But I hardly ever see them even when I'm home. My wife got full custody because of my job. One week a year and Saturdays when I'm on leave. That's all I got. I just seem to be a nuisance and an interruption when I go to visit."

He looked Sally in the eye. She sensed a real sadness behind the bullish self-confidence. Sally reached out and touched his hand. There was that electricity again. The one she had felt with Jon. She wasn't cheating on him. He had made his position clear.

This was a more familiar current. It reminded her of steamed up car windows or tangled arms and legs on the tatty double bed in her parents' caravan. She slowly wrapped her fingers around his, anticipating the warmth of his breath as they leant in closer.

She was captivated by George and the memories he brought back so vividly. She barely registered the lights in the club changing, Stephen moving away from the table or Josie checking if she wanted to share the taxi home and winking when they left without her.

She had lost track of how many cocktails she had consumed. She felt like she was riding on the crest of a wave, with no concern for how she might come down again. Then the club was closing and they were being ushered out.

"Let's not end the evening here," said George. "I'm staying at The Smythson Hotel next door. Come for a drink."

This was George. How could Sally refuse him? Why would she want to?

***

The mother's day...

Someone was gently tugging on Sally's hand. She had been dreaming. She was sure of that. But she couldn't remember what about. Now she was in that soft space between sleep and waking. Sensing but not quite feeling. There it was again. The tugging. She forced herself through a fog of cotton wool and opened her eyes.

Lizzy was standing at the side of the bed. She was in her night dress. She stretched out her arm and proudly presented her mum with a bunch of flowers. Daffodils. Three.

"Happy Mummy's Day." she said. "I got you these."

Sally sat up and took the yellow blooms. Her favourite. The front garden was full of these at this time of year.

"They're lovely, Lizzy. But where..."

Sally was wide awake. She jumped out of bed and ran to the top of the stairs. A kitchen stool was sitting in the middle of the hallway. The front door was slightly ajar.

"I picked them. From the garden." Lizzy's voice was trembling. "Don't you like them?"

Sally fixed a smile on her face and turned around to look directly at her three-year-old daughter. Lizzy had been trying to be good. Even if that had meant letting herself outside at – what time was it? – seven o'clock in the morning. Telling her about the dangers was for later. So too was pointing out that garden flowers were not for picking.

"They're beautiful," she said. "You're such a good girl. Thank you." She picked Lizzy up and hugged her tight.

It was Damien she should be cross with. Every Father's Day and birthday since he left she had made sure the children had a card to give him. Not for his benefit. For Jack and Lizzy. Because they wanted to give him a card. And he had always made such a fuss. He had not once reciprocated.

Just last month, Sally had been shopping with Jack. At his insistence she had helped him find *Mummy's Birthday* cards on a stall in the parade. He had asked her for some money. Then he had told her to go away.

From a safe distance, she had seen him queue and pay. Then he came skipping towards her. Delighted with his purchase hidden inside the paper bag he was holding so tightly.

But she was not perfect. She had to admit that. If only to herself. She gained a perverse pleasure in buying Damien presents from the children that he and Sharon would hate.

Her greatest triumph was a hideous fluffy dog remote control holder. It was designed to hang over the arm of a chair or sofa. A remote in each ear. It would have completely spoiled Sharon's beautiful décor. Sally was sure it would not feature in Good Homes magazine. She should feel a little bit bad. She didn't.

***

They entered the hotel lobby. Sally turned towards the bar. George gently put his hands round her waist. He steered her in a different direction. Towards the lifts.

"Let's raid my mini bar. I've got a suite. We'll be more comfortable in there," he said.

Sally watched the numbers of the floors flash from ten to one on the wall in front of them, as the lift approached the ground floor. The doors opened slowly, invitingly. She hesitated. George looked at her expectantly. She stepped in. George followed. They were alone. Surrounded by mirrors. She watched him pull her closer. He lowered his head.

"You smell fantastic," he whispered in her ear. "I want to eat you up."

Sally doubted this kind of sweet talk was in the Captains' training manual.

On the tenth floor they stepped out of the lift and into the hotel corridor. They walked, hand in hand. Silent. Sally felt a mixture of fear and excitement. Could she even remember how this worked? George clearly had more recent practice. He had barely opened his room door when he pulled her into his arms, kissed her forcefully and placed her onto the bed.

He lay down next to her and started to run his hands along her back. Kissing her mouth, face and neck.

"You do want this don't you?" he said.

Sally nodded. She stopped thinking. Her body seemed to naturally remember the shape of George. As if an impression had been left on her brain and stored for future use. She let him undo the buttons of her dress and pull it gently away from her tingling skin. He stood up in front of her and confidently took his clothes off. Each item was removed slowly, folded and put onto a chair, until he was completely naked.

She expected him to return to her on the bed. Instead he opened his wardrobe door and reached for something. Condoms? She had not thought about contraception at all. How stupid. Just because it was George didn't mean she could forget everything else. She still needed to stay safe. At least he was being careful. Wasn't he?

"The ladies love this," said George, putting on his peaked captain's hat with a theatrical flourish.

Sally was speechless. It didn't matter. A loud hotel fire alarm drowned out anything she might have said.

Cocktails

Your Shopping List
Whatever cocktail you fancy.

How to make it
Don't bother. Just buy and drink.

Chapter Nine

People were walking down the corridor. They were talking loudly. Excitedly. Someone was banging on each hotel room door. Theirs was no exception.

"Fire! Fire! Please leave your room and go to the assembly point," said a disembodied voice.

They opened the door. The smell of smoke instantly hit them. This was clearly not a drill.

"Bugger!" said George, closing the door again. "We better go."

They dressed quickly, then joined a queue of people making their way to the stairs. Sally wished she had worn something far more sensible on her feet than the three-inch heels that had seemed such a good idea eight hours before.

George took her hand. An image of their charred bodies being found huddled together forced itself onto her. What would her children think? She walked faster, ignoring the pain in the soles of her feet.

They were on the fourth floor. A strange sense of quiet panic had taken hold of nearly all the guests snaking their way down the concrete steps. They were terrified but holding it together. Just. After what felt like an hour but was probably only a few minutes, they reached the open fire door and escaped into the car park. There was a collective gasp of relief as they filed out.

George was looking back at the hotel. She followed his gaze. A fire had properly taken hold on the top floor. Flames were bursting out of the windows and licking the roof above. Two fire engines were pulling up and the crew were jumping from the cabs. A man with a yellow high visibility jacket walked past.

"Are there still people in there?" George asked.

The hotel employee George had addressed did a double take. George was still wearing his cap. Along with an unbuttoned, crisp white captain's shirt, with four stripes on each shoulder, and clearly mismatched trousers.

"No, we don't think so. It started in the manager's rooms and he's away. All the floors have been cleared."   His words tumbled out, as if they too were trying to escape the fire. Then the man turned his attention to a noisy crowd of people further down the car park.

Sally let go of George's hand.

"Is it obvious what we've been doing?"

George laughed. "I think it's obvious what most people have been doing," he said. "It's Saturday night. We're all here for pleasure not business."

He looked down at himself. "Perhaps I had important cruise ship business to attend to."

"Here?" Sally laughed. What else could she do?

George took off his cap. He looked at it then put it back on his head again. "I was focussed on saving you," he said, as he did up his shirt buttons.

She was cold. It was three in the morning. The fire and being outside had sobered her up. She needed to go home. She didn't want anyone to know she had been here. With George. Damien would be asleep on the sofa. He would see her creep in. She shouldn't care about that. For some reason she did. What if the children woke up? Her phone beeped loudly. Who would be calling her now?

She pulled her mobile out of the small glittery clutch bag she had borrowed from Lizzy. She had not remembered picking that up when they left the room in such a hurry. She was glad she had. How would she have explained its loss? *'Rach'* was illuminated across the screen. She swiped across.

***

The loneliness…

Sally tucked Jack into bed again. She had to get up for work in three hours. Her eyes were heavy. Jack's were wide open. He had woken her up several times already. She felt like her patience was a stretched elastic band. Ready to snap at any moment.

It was in these moments that she felt the most alone. What she would give for someone by her side, sharing the burden. To talk. To fill the empty spaces and shadows in her house and in her heart. To free her from the knowledge that this was now her lot.

This was what being a lone parent really meant. How she wished she could show those misguided people who said they understood. Just because their husbands or partners were away sometimes. Who believed they had insight into the deep, dark well of loneliness she could fall into at night. She closed her eyes. Perhaps she might be able to fall asleep again after all.

"Bear's on fire!"

Sally jumped up. Jack was in the doorway. She rushed into the bedroom. Jack ran in behind her. She could smell smoke. Lizzy was asleep on the bottom bunk. The three-foot polar bear Damien had bought Jack the year before to replace a promised holiday was smouldering on the top bed. Its head was pushed up against the wall lamp. Sally pulled it away. One of its ears had melted.

Without thinking she picked up the soft toy and carried it into the bathroom. She put it in the bath and turned on the shower. Cold water poured onto the blackened fabric.

"I think he's lost his good looks," she said, giving her distressed son a hug.

"He will still be Bear though won't he?" said Jack.

****

Rachel was gabbling.

"Oh Sally, I'm so glad you're ok because Stephen told us earlier he and George were staying at the Smythson and then I was awake with the twins and I

151

saw the fire on social media and I was worried you might be there so I texted you but you didn't reply and I didn't want to wake you but I just couldn't stop worrying, I'm so glad you're ok, you are ok aren't you?"

Sally took an urgent breath of air, even though she had not been the one speaking.

"Yes, I'm fine. I am at the Smythson. We're in the car park. The fire's bad but they think everyone's out."

"Oh, thank God for that. Look, Karl can come and get you. You can't stay there all night."

"Really? That would be great. If you're sure."

"Of course, I'm sure. He'll text you when he's nearby. Should be about fifteen minutes."

Sally turned to George. "I've got a friend coming to pick me up," she said. "Will you be ok?"

"Yes," he replied. "My car's here somewhere. I'll find Stephen and then we'll drive to my brother's. It's not far from here."

"Why didn't you stay with him in the first place?"

"In case I got lucky."

Sally wondered if the fire meant SHE had.

Her eyes were drawn to something happening to her left. A man she could only see in profile seemed to be taking command of the situation. He looked familiar.

"Can we get a shot of the hotel sign from here? Then I'll do a piece to camera."

It was Jon. He was standing just ten yards away with his side kick Simon. She was pretty sure he

152

hadn't seen her yet. But it was only a matter of time if she stayed where she was.

"I'm going to wait for my friend over there," she said to George, walking away before she finished talking.

Her shoes were hurting even more now. And slowing her down. She needed to walk the length of the car park to the main road. She took them off and speeded up. Her heart was beating fast. She was not sure how much more it could take. Life was much simpler, much better, when Saturday nights consisted of X Factor on the television and an Indian takeaway.

And she had crossed one of Josie's red lines. She had let her illicit life overlap with her routine one. What was the acronym Josie had invented? Hexagon? This was more of a palindrome. Whichever way you looked at it, she had made a mess of things.

Sally looked back. To where she had been waiting a few moments before. She could hardly believe her eyes. Jon was standing in front of George with a microphone pointed in his direction. They were both illuminated in a ring of bright light. George was talking animatedly. Waving his arms around. His cap still on his head.

Sally had done those short interviews with random members of the public. She had usually avoided anyone who looked even slightly odd. George would have certainly fallen into that category.

What if George said he was with someone? Please don't let him say her name. What if he turned around to point her out in the crowd? If she could see them, they would be able to see her.

She needed to get out of their line of sight. Fast. She saw a gap in the hedge surrounding the tarmacked spaces. She squeezed in. There was just enough room. Brambles scratched at her legs. She prayed to the god of awkward that no one would see her here. Her phone beeped loudly and lit up again.

It's Karl. I'm parked on the road. The other side of the hedge.

She turned. There was Karl's car. The headlights illuminating her escape route. It took a good two minutes to battle through the knotted shrubbery to where he was waiting.

Despite it all, she had never been so pleased to see him. To see anyone. He leant across the passenger seat and opened her door. She got in and immediately fastened her seat belt. Kar's car felt familiar and safe.

"You ok?" said Karl, a smile playing on the edge of his lips.

"I am now! Thank you."

"No problem." Karl put the car into gear and pulled away. Ten minutes later, he was driving into the street that ran directly behind his house. He parked in front of his garage and unlocked the gate into his garden.

"Thought you might want to be incognito," he teased.

Sally was too grateful and too tired to respond. She followed Karl up the path. Even in the dark she could make out the beautifully manicured lawn and blossoming flowerbeds. Apart from the ready-planted pots her mum provided, Sally's garden was only grass and obstinate weeds. It all seemed to come so easily to others.

"Sally! Come on in." Rachel was standing in her back doorway. She had clearly been keeping an eye out for her friend.

"I've just been making some cupcakes. Do you want one?"

Karl looked at his wife, the love between them shining out of his eyes. "At four in the morning," he said. "Perfectly normal behaviour."

***

The rat poison…

"Can I have some chocolate please Mummy?"

"I don't have any Lizzy. And you haven't had your breakfast yet."

"Jack's eating some. And he won't let me have any."

"Jack doesn't have any chocolate."

"He does. He's eating it in bed."

Sally took the stairs two steps at a time. What

was Jack eating? There was no chocolate in the house. Only a few Maltesers.

Maltesers she had found in a tatty old box. A box that was hiding under the settee. The settee she had pulled away from the wall to clean the floor. The floor where she had spilt some rat poison. Some poison she had bought to kill the creatures in the garage. The garage where she kept her outside bin. Her outside bin into which she had thrown the poison and the Maltesers.

Jack was sitting on the top bunk. He was at head height. The evidence was overwhelming. He had chocolate all over his face and on his pyjamas. Sally could feel a volcano of panic start to rumble inside her. She tried to push it back down before the larva burst through and erupted out of her mouth in loud breathless shouts.

"Jack! What have you done! Where did you get that chocolate from? Was it in the bin? You silly boy!"

She pulled him off the bed. She had read somewhere about drinking milk to combat poison. Or was it salt water to make them sick? She couldn't remember. She rang her mum. As she always did when her brain lost the ability to think straight. When she was on the edge of the abyss.

"Calm down Sally. You need to ring 111. I'm sure he'll be fine. Did he definitely get it out of the bin? Why would he do such a thing? Don't worry. Your dad and I will come round now."

Fifteen minutes later, Sally had rung NHS Direct and was feeling slightly calmer. At least her thoughts were less tangled. Jack had been adamant that he had eaten only Maltesers. Not the 'funny blue tablets'. Her parents' car pulled up onto the drive. She bent to put her head near the open passenger window.

"The nurse said as long as he didn't swallow any actual rat poison he should be fine. We just need to keep an eye on him."

"Well your dad will stay with him in the car for a while. It's not worth getting his wheelchair out. He can watch for symptoms. Let's go in the house and have a coffee. I know I need one."

"Thanks, Dad," Sally said. "I'll bring a coffee out for you too."

She called Jack. He appeared quickly. His eyes were red from crying. "I'm sorry Mummy. I was hungry."

"It's ok. Go and play with Grandad. He wants to check you're alright."

Jack loved spending time with Sally's father. He climbed eagerly into the car. Sally noticed he was still in his pyjamas. She would let that one go.

Jack and her dad stayed in the car all morning. Every time Sally checked, the two generations were happily engaged in each other's company. Jack had never asked why his grandad couldn't walk. Why would he? Her father resolutely refused to be defined by the multiple sclerosis that had first reared its ugly head when she was four years old.

She brought out coffee, squash, biscuits, lunch. It became clear there was nothing to be worried about, other than her mum's reaction to the mess in the car when they left.

***

The twins were at the table in their highchairs. From the cream on their faces and the crumbs on the floor beneath them, they had clearly already started on the cupcakes.

Rachel busied herself at the kitchen worktop. "Joe and Sam wouldn't go back to sleep once they heard Karl get up," she said.

"They can always sense when something exciting's happening. Unlike their mother who's not made an appearance outside her room since ten last night. I just gave up on the idea of sleep and started cooking. It calms me down."

Sally was impressed at Rachel's self-control. She was sure she would have interrogated her friend, had the tables been turned. Karl walked over to his wife and took one of the few cupcakes that had already been iced. He ate it in two bites, then stretched out his sticky hands and simultaneously ruffled his grandchildren's hair.

"Karl!" Rachel chided her husband. She gave him a playful slap and was kissed on the top of her head in reply.

"You offered one to Sally," he said. "And I should be in your good books after my derring-do rescue of a damsel in distress."

"I'm very grateful," said Sally, taking a cup of hot coffee from Rachel.

"No need," said Karl. "I'm looking forward to hearing the full story of how you ended up in our kitchen at this early hour, in last night's clothes."

Rachel wacked him with her tea towel. "Karl! Get straight to the point why don't you!"

"My ability to see what is right in front of me is one of the reasons you love me so much. And why I am so good at my job."

"Does being an accountant also require being a bit of a dick? Go away. Sally and I need to talk."

Karl grabbed another cup cake and walked outside. The sun was just starting to reveal the colours of the garden. Karl seated himself at the patio table, deliberately close enough to be within earshot of any conversation in the kitchen.

Rachel slid the patio doors shut. "Sorry, Sally, he can be a right nuisance!"

"Now, if you don't fancy a cupcake, I could make you some beans on toast."

Beans on toast

Your Shopping List
1. One tin baked beans
2. Two slices bread
3. Butter

How to make
1. Toast bread
2. Butter bread
3. Heat beans on the hob or in the microwave and pour over toast

Chapter Ten

"Just passing through! Have you got to the good bit yet?"

Karl noisily entered and exited the kitchen, as if he were in a stage play and had been waiting excitedly for his cue. Sally had been in her friends' house for more than an hour. She hadn't slept for twenty. She was acutely aware she had done all the talking. While Rachel did her best to keep the twins occupied, fed, and some way towards clean.

"Sorry Rachel, I've been babbling on. And I've kept you awake all night."

"You haven't kept me awake. Joe and Sam have. Anyway, just because I'm not as crass as Karl to ask, doesn't mean I don't want you to tell me all your gossip. Your life's getting very exciting all of a sudden."

"Not sure 'exciting' is the word I'd use," said Sally. "Who was it who said that men are like buses? You wait ages and then three come along at once. And in my case they're all a Mystery Tour."

Rachel picked up Joe and put his nappy to her face, grimacing as she did so. "I've gone right off mysteries since these two came on the scene."

Despite their close friendship, Sally had not heard Rachel talk directly about the twins' unexpected arrival before. Unanswered questions hung in the air.

"I wish Laura had told me earlier that she was pregnant. I had assumed we shared everything. I was always here for both the girls. But then I didn't notice and she didn't say. Made me think perhaps we weren't as strong a family unit as I believed we were.

"Even now, she still won't tell me who their dad is. She hadn't ever had a boyfriend as far as I was aware. I assumed at first that he might be in the sixth form with her and she was embarrassed. Especially as he clearly wanted nothing to do with them. But she's been left two years now. It's selfish, I know, but a bit more money and other people to share the load with would be very helpful. And I don't know what we'll do if Kate comes back home to stay after university."

Rachel put Joe under her left arm and pulled the changing mat from a gap between the kitchen cupboards with her free hand.

"And we could have discussed... other options. We wouldn't be without them now of course. You know that. They're our world. And there's no question how much Laura loves them. But she isn't ready to be a mum. She still wants to be a teenager. Going out. Having fun."

Karl joined them again with the same impeccable timing.

"I've just been up to Laura's room to tell her it was about time she took over from you," he said sharply. "I'm sure there's a man in there!"

162

Rachel sighed. "Looks like it'll be me sorting out this dirty bottom then," she said. As much to her grandson as to her husband.

"Don't you care?" said Karl, his voice trembling. "Who do you think it is? Do you think he's been here all night?"

Rachel's tone changed. Sally noticed an almost imperceptible stiffening of her friend's body.

"I don't know who it is Karl, or how long they've been up there. It's a bit too late to be worrying about what our daughter's getting up to. Don't you think?"

It was time Sally left. How she was going to explain her very late - or very early - appearance to Damien and the children? Perhaps she should say she had come back to Rachel's after the club. That she had drunk so much she had passed out on their sofa bed. It was worrying that Damien and the children were likely to accept this, without comment.

All five heads in the kitchen turned. Someone was knocking on the front door.

"It's six in the morning! Who calls round at six o'clock in the morning?" said Karl.

Rachel was on her hands and knees on the floor, wrestling with a wriggling child and an obstinate box of baby wipes. Joe started weeing onto his grandmother, giggling as though they were playing a great game.

"Why don't you answer it and find out?" she said without lifting her head. Dealing with out of control bodily fluids was clearly not improving her mood.

Karl was already walking through the hall. Sally heard him open the door.

"Josie! Hi! Come in. Welcome to the world's earliest coffee morning."

There was a pause. Karl audibly softened. "Are you ok? Rachel and Sally are through there."

Josie walked into the kitchen looking upset. "Is Andrew here? He wasn't in his bed when I got back last night and he's still not home."

Rachel got back up on her feet. She returned Joe to his high chair, before washing her hands in the sink.

"I'm sure he's ok," she said. "He's probably just out with friends."

Josie shook her head.

"He doesn't seem to have any friends. Not around here anyway. He talked to me yesterday. I had no idea he was so unhappy. His studies are getting him down and he's split up with his girlfriend. He says he doesn't want to go back to university."

Sally offered Josie a seat next to her at the table. "What, never?"

"Well, certainly not this week. He was supposed to be in Leeds three days ago. I was afraid something was wrong and I've tried talking to him but until yesterday he just shut me out. I didn't want to leave him last night but he insisted I shouldn't let you two down. Now he's disappeared."

"No, he hasn't."

Karl was standing in the kitchen doorway. Andrew was just behind him, bedraggled and half asleep.

"He's the man in Laura's bedroom. I didn't bother knocking this time."

***

The viewing…

Sally looked around her. She was pleased with her efforts. She had spent the last few hours tidying and cleaning the house. It looked shiny and smelt of lemon.

She had left work early in order to grab a couple of hours without the children. The irony that precious time to herself was being used to crouch on her knees with a cloth in her hand was not lost on her. Nor that she was both performing the task at hand and at the same time incurring the cost of childcare. She could have just paid a cleaner and spent the time with the kids. But she was pleased with the transformation she had achieved. It had needed doing properly. And by her.

She wanted the people viewing the house that evening to fall in love with it as she had. To see its potential as a happy home. She and Damien had bought it new with a hundred per cent mortgage and high hopes. It was entirely her property now. Well, hers and the bank's.

Through gritted teeth, her dad had written Damien a cheque for £4,000. Replacing the savings Damien had built up before they got married and that they had used to furnish the house. It meant she would get any profit from a sale. She would be forever grateful to her parents for that. And for so much more.

She was ready to move on. Yes, she wanted to live somewhere that had no bad memories or thoughts of might-have-beens but there were practical reasons too. Jack and Lizzy could not share a bedroom forever. And growing children needed a bigger garden.

The children would have to be picked up soon. Giving them their tea and getting them ready for bed would mean having to tidy up all over again before the estate agent and potential buyers walked through the door. It was not ideal. She had no choice.

Three hours later, everything was going to plan. Apart from the children's mood. She had imagined them calmly watching something on television while the visitors toured the house. Instead they had sensed the air of anticipation and were more awake than normal. They were unable to sit still.

"Behave!" Sally shouted to Jack and Lizzy as the doorbell rang. "You need to be good tonight. Please!"

Jack giggled loudly, pushing Lizzy off the sofa where she had been perching precariously, causing her to howl in surprise or pain. Their two cats, named Fizz and Milo by the children after characters in one of their favourite television programmes, looked up briefly from their spot near the fire. Sally hoped they at least would make the place seem more homely.

She stepped back to let the three people waiting in the porch through into the hall.

"I'm afraid my children are still wide awake. But they have been told to be on their best behaviour."

"Yes. Well." said the male half of what she assumed to be a couple. This was not an encouraging start.

She returned to the living room and gave Jack and Lizzy what she hoped was one of her scariest stares.

It was probably best she let the estate agent do the tour.

"Mrs Stainton?" said the agent from the landing, five minutes later. "Would you mind just showing us the inside of the wardrobes?"

She let the 'Mrs' error go. It was a frequent mistake. She was much more concerned by the request for her to open her wardrobe doors. She had not expected that. It was where she had stuffed everything that didn't have an obvious home. At least they'd be able to see just how much you could fit in there.

She reached the bedroom and slid the wardrobe doors to the left. The woman looked inside and then at her male companion. It was hard to miss the disapproval on her face.

The house erupted with noise. Jack was running up the stairs. He was holding Rabbit and Doll. Lizzy was chasing him. Both were shouting at the top of their voices.

Jack ran into Sally's bedroom. Lizzy was one step behind him. She grabbed for Rabbit, missed and pulled at her brother's pyjama trousers. They came down to his ankles. He dropped the treasured cuddly toy and pulled her trousers down in revenge. They rolled around on the floor. As good as naked from the waist down. Oblivious to everything and everyone around them.

"STOP IT!" Sally wrestled them apart. Then held them. One in each arm. She looked up at her open-mouthed audience.

"I think we've seen enough," said the man. "This isn't what we're looking for, thank you." The visitors squeezed past Sally, who had pulled herself and her now subdued children towards the wall and made their way outside.

Ten minutes later, the house was quiet. The children were in bed. Sally was weeping in the living room. Why was it all so hard? The children were supposed to be on her side. They might be small, but they had crossed a line. Enough was enough.

***

Andrew was shifting from foot to foot. He was clearly not keen to remain under his mother's gaze a moment longer than necessary.

"I'm sorry mum. I should have left a note. You really don't have to worry about me. I'm not going to do anything stupid."

"Well I was worried," said Josie. "You better get off home. I'll be there in a minute."

Andrew did not need to be told twice.

Josie looked like she might cry.

"Have a cup of coffee before you go back," said Rachel, putting the kettle on again.

"I didn't expect him to be here," said Josie. "But I supposed Laura might know where he was. They've always been so close. And they're friends on all the social media. He sounded so low yesterday. My mind was running wild."

"Have you talked to his dad about it?" said Sally.

"Oh, he's *'working away'*." Josie drew quote marks in the air. "That usually means he's on some exotic holiday with *'the secretary',*" More quote marks were required. "Or on the golf course. Either way he's as much use as a crochet condom."

Rachel put the steaming mugs on the table.

"Which I hope is NOT what Andrew and Laura were using," she said with one eye on the twins.

A rare look of shock crossed Josie's face. Sally needed to distract her.

"Andrew and Richard get on better than most brothers I know. Have you talked to him?"

Josie picked up her coffee and took a sip. "He's so busy at work."

"You should ask him to help. He won't mind."

"Have a cupcake first though," said Rachel, offering Josie the tray.

Josie took a cake and looked at Sally as if she were seeing her properly for the first time that morning.

"What are you doing here? This doesn't bode well for meeting last night's objective."

Sally was saved by the beeps. It was her phone. A Facebook request from George. He wanted to send her a direct message. She accepted. Her phone beeped again.

Karl was ensconced back in the kitchen. He had clearly decided he was not prepared to miss any more of the action. Sally read the message out loud to her assembled audience.

Hi Sally, sorry I was a bit of an arse last night. It really was good to see you. I'm going back to my ship tomorrow. Could I give you a call when I'm next on shore leave?

"He WAS a bit of an arse," said Sally.

"He does have a nice arse," said Josie.

"That's the problem. I still fancy him as much as I did when we were teenagers. But I think perhaps we didn't work for a reason."

Sally tapped into her phone.

It was good to see you too. I think every 20 years is probably about right though.

"Harsh." said Karl, looking over her shoulder. "Not his fault you had to do the walk of shame. And it was only through our garden."

"I've still got to get home," said Sally.

"Wear some of my clothes," said Rachel. "Say you got up early and came over here."

"I've clearly missed all the excitement. I must be losing my touch," said Josie.

Ten minutes later Sally was putting the key in her front door. Maybe everyone would still be in bed. The blaring television in the living room told her otherwise. She started to creep up the stairs. Lizzy came out of her bedroom and walked across the landing. Sally stayed still. Her daughter closed the bathroom door behind her. Sally sighed with relief, continuing silently towards her own room.

Her daughter's voice rang out. "Rachel's got that top."

***

The stand…

Working full time meant Sally could not be waiting at the school gates to deposit or collect the children. She was not part of any of the huddles of mums arranging whose house they would go to for coffee afterwards. She barely knew any of the other parents.

The Parent Teacher Association had been a good way to make connections. But she had little time to spare. She had gone to the recruitment drive masked as a cheese and wine evening just to be polite, to listen and find out what it was all about. Perhaps offer to help out occasionally. Lots of other parents would be there, keener and more able than her to actually join.

She remembered walking into the school hall. Was she early? At a table in front of the stage three women and a man were talking. In front of them were rows of chairs. Enough for thirty to forty parents. Only three of them were occupied. And by people who seemed to have chosen their seats based on a mathematical equation that placed them exactly equidistant from each other.

Sally's grade C 'O' level maths could not stretch to that and she sat down next to the friendliest face.

The woman, who Sally faintly recognized, turned to her and smiled. "If more people don't arrive soon the

Chair will have you on the committee. I've come to resign. I've done my bit.

"Oh, I'm not joining," said Sally, "It's my first meeting."

"We must both stand firm then."

Half an hour later, the reappointed Treasurer had introduced herself to the new Publicity Officer. Josie and Sally commiserated with each other over a glass of wine in a flimsy plastic cup, a stale cracker and some rubbery cheddar. All served by the Head who was barely keeping her eyes open after yet another 12-hour-day.

Nearly a year later, Sally was committed. She extracted a bright yellow apron out of the dressing up box and tied it round her waist. She rummaged for the pound shop Easter bonnet. There it was, squashed out of shape, each of the fluffy chicks hanging on by a thread. She pulled it down hard on her larger than normal head. All the Staintons suffered in the same way. Physically rather than metaphorically, of course. Hats were not their thing.

She was not aiming to look good today though. And if you were going to look bad, it was helpful if people could tell you had tried.

It was not enough that she had designed and distributed the posters. All the members of the PTA, with nothing better to do on a Saturday than manage a stand at their child's primary school Easter fair, had been expressly asked to look the part by the Chair, a formidable woman you did not mess with lightly. Sally took a pair of fake easter egg earrings out of a drawer and put them on.   She wrapped some yellow ribbon round her neck as her coup de grace, before walking into the living room.

"What do you think?"

Her mum looked up from the board game she was playing – and certainly winning - with Jack and Lizzy.

"Are you sure?"

Sally looked down at the headless chicken now strutting across her chest.

"I think it's rather me."

"I meant are you really not going to take the children?"

"No. I am not. They need to understand."

Her children looked at her pleadingly. Then they looked at their grandma. Then back to their mum. They had clearly been hoping for a volte-face. Another good French expression. All those years of study really had been worth it.

"Well you're a stronger woman than me. Just look at their little faces"

Sally had deliberately not looked at Jack and Lizzy's little faces in the last thirty minutes. They had been shocked and upset that her chosen punishment was to leave them behind, following the 'pyjama incident' as the house viewing embarrassment was now known.

There was no doubt where grandma's allegiances lay. Sally indicated for her to come into the kitchen.

"I can't keep forgiving them everything because their dad left," said Sally. "What kind of people will they grow up to be?"

"Well you know I will always support you," said her mum. "But this does seem hard for them."

"It's supposed to be."

Sally was not sure whose heart was breaking the most as she drove away from home. Her own, or those of her children staring longingly out of the front window.

****

Sally had stayed in bed most of the day. She had not slept at all the night before. She was tired. And she wanted to avoid any awkward conversations. She had been left alone. Now, however, she was being bothered by the tell-tale aroma of a late Sunday dinner with all the trimmings. She was really hungry. The food would be good. But she didn't fancy sitting around the dining table being questioned about the night before.

She was idly looking at her phone, trying to distract herself, when a message came through from Josie.

How are you doing? Fancy some hair of the dog round mine? I've got a curry on the go. Chicken Tikka Masala.

Sally replied.

Yes please. You're a life saver. I'll be there in five mins.

She didn't bother to wash. That would take too long. She threw on some clothes and ran down the stairs. She paused at the front door.

"I'm just popping out!" she shouted to anyone who might be listening. She was out of range by the time they might have replied.

Josie had left the door on the latch.

"Come through! Your fire's on the news. Rachel told me ALL about it!"

Josie's 55-inch-screen, bought as a treat for her boys when they were 18 and 21 within a few weeks of each other, dominated the room. A newsreader was sitting at a desk with a picture of the burnt-out hotel behind them. Josie turned up the volume.

"The fire broke out shortly before 3am, ripping through the historic Smythson Hotel and causing guests to be evacuated from their rooms. The blaze started in the manager's living quarters. No one was hurt but millions of pounds of damage was caused to the Grade One listed building. Our reporter Jon Oldman was on the scene."

There was Jon. In the car park. Last night. The huge television made him appear almost life-size.

"The Smythson Hotel is owned by Crown Cruises tycoon, Jeremy Toffington," he said.

Crown Cruises? Where had Sally heard that before?

"The captain of one of his ships, George Turner, was staying here and was in his hotel room when the fire broke out. He joins me now. George. How are you feeling?"

"It's awful. I've stayed here lots of times. We get a great discount."

"And what were you doing when the fire alarm went off?"

Sally put her hands to her mouth.

George paused. The corners of his mouth twitched. It was a tiny gesture which would not have been visible on an ordinary-sized screen.

"I was ironing my uniform. I heard the alarm and threw it on. This cap is my lucky charm. Had it since I passed my exams."

Jon turned back to face the camera. And Sally.

"Well, a cap seems to have been lucky for one guest, if not for the poor old Smythson. Jon Oldman, at the Smythson Hotel, Look Midlands."

"Let's see that again," said Josie. "This is priceless."

"What kind of a friend are you?" said Sally.

"A friend who knows when to milk a good opportunity for a laugh," said Josie. "Just once more. Then I'll feed you. I promise."

Sally sat down on the sofa. It might be easier to watch this time. Now she knew what was coming.

The introduction. Then Jon. Now George was talking again.

"That's you!" Josie started jumping up and down in front of the television. "I recognise your dress. There in the background. Running away! Oh Sally, this just keeps getting better!"

Sally wasn't sure Josie's curry was going to be worth this humiliation.

"Maybe I'm just not meant to have sex ever again," said Sally, tucking into her tea half an hour later.

Josie started waving her naan bread around. Bits of chicken were flying across the table.

"You are meant to have sex. You're just doing it wrong! Well, not the sex, obviously. You aren't having any. I mean the way you're approaching this whole thing. You're confusing lust with love. If it's lust you're in control. If it's love then it gets complicated."

Sally bit into a bay leaf. She never understood why they were there when you weren't supposed to eat them.

"I just don't want to die a bitter and twisted old hag. What if I have the menopause and lose interest before anything ever happens?"

"Firstly, the menopause does not automatically mean you lose interest. Secondly, and I repeat what I just said, lust puts you in control."

"What do you mean?"

"Isn't it obvious? If you want love you have to meet a man you really like. He has to really like you. Then you have to spend ages getting to know each other properly and deciding if he truly is a good human being or a wolf in disguise. On the way, you meet his friends and family and get tangled up with them as well. Sex is complicated because it means something.

Josie paused. She fetched another bottle from her fridge. She poured herself and Sally a drink. Sally drained her whole glass. All 250ml.

"Alternatively, if you stick to lust, you can meet a man, have fantastic sex, feel good about yourself, say goodbye, move on to the next one."

Sally put down her knife and fork.

"Josie, that is one warped view of the world."

Josie did not wait for her mouth to be empty of food.

"Is it? Make your choice. I have."

Sally wasn't sure she could choose. Although something told her she should be wherever Josie was.

Chicken Tikka Masala

Your Shopping List
1.   One 420g Jar Tikka Masala Medium Sauce
2.   3-4 diced chicken breasts

How to make
1.   Fry 3-4 diced chicken breasts in a little oil until browned.
2.   Add the sauce and simmer for a few more minutes until all is cooked through.

Ensure food is fully cooked and piping hot before serving.

Serves 4

Serve with rice, naans and mango chutney

Chapter Eleven

The three women scrambled out of the taxi. Nearly tripping over each other's coats and shoes. High on the excitement of a day off together. Josie was craning her neck to take in the whole of Montgomery Hall.

"Well. It certainly looks like it's going to live up to our expectations."

The spa had promised perfect pampering. They had agreed on the way there that they deserved nothing less.

"Let's go and see," said Sally. "Our facials await."

"And our massages and barefoot therapies," added Rachel.

Sally wasn't sure about that last one. She had walked over enough hot coals recently.

The three friends instinctively linked arms. They walked up the granite steps and through the grand entrance. The inside of the building looked like an expensive private hospital. Staff were in purple, clinical, uniforms. Many were holding clipboards or talking to visitors. Sally had not been to a spa in years. She been to the Spar lots of times, emergency shopping for the kid's tea.

She had almost forgotten to claim her competition prize. She had been distracted. The voucher sat on the bookcase by the door from the moment it arrived, quickly disappearing under a growing pile of 'recycling'.

She had come across it when she was looking for a school letter for Lizzy. Email was so much better. She could look through that on work's time. She could give it a flag or even a sound. She could make it appear on her desktop. She could not trust herself to remember everything but she could trust her computer to remind her. She liked to think of Bill Gates as her PA, though she wished it were Steve Jobs.

When she read the voucher properly, she saw that it was only valid for a month. It was a short window of opportunity but she could hardly complain. Other than the shame, it had cost her nothing. It reminded her of the freebies she'd received as a journalist – the best part of the job.

The prize was for two. With a third person at half price. The accompanying leaflet carried images of tempting discounted cocktails. Josie would be keen to take advantage of those. And it made sense to ask Rachel too, to thank her for the other night. She would be reluctant to leave the twins all day though. Sally would have to remind her yet again that Laura was their mother.

"Ladies! Ladies! Come this way!"

A well-manicured woman, her age masked by heavy make-up, started shepherding them to the front desk. Sally handed her the voucher she had been holding in her hand.

"Our competition winners! How exciting!"

They were guided by the same woman through a green velvet curtain to the right of the reception area. Behind the enormous, thick, drapes was a sumptuous room. Decorative throws and cushions were artistically scattered across three grand settees and a chaise longue. A huge mirror hung on the wall. Sally gasped. It looked so inviting. Once she sat down she might never get up again. Perhaps she wouldn't bother with the treatments after all.

"Exclusively yours for the day!"

The woman appeared only able to speak in exclamations.

"And one of you must be Sally! How exciting! We've all been talking about you! 14 years! How do you do it?"

"Or don't do it," laughed Josie, identifying Sally with a nudge of her elbow. "She's putting herself out there again now. So, all is not lost. There's still hope."

"In that case, I shall add a bikini wax to your treatments! On the house!"

This was not Sally's idea of fun. Was it too early to raid the mini bar she had noticed in the corner of the room?

"I'll be back in five minutes with your treatment plans! Make yourselves at home!"

Rachel threw herself into a chaise longue and melted into the cushions. Sally and Josie opened a door at the back of the room. Directly opposite the curtains they had come through. It led to a sauna, hot tub and cold plunge pool.

"Thanks Sally. This is possibly the best birthday present I've ever had. And it's not even my birthday," said Josie.

"I can't believe they've been discussing my love life."

"Twitter is discussing your love life. You've gone viral."

"I hope not!"

"At least it's only an online virus! And if you'd had sex since Tony Blair became Prime Minister we wouldn't be here. As far as I can see, celibacy is underrated."

***

The move...

The children were being slow. They needed a push to get them through the gates. Being taken to school by their mum was usually a treat. And she would get pleasure from watching them walking into the playground. Sometimes she would even have time to talk to the few other mums that she recognized from PTA committees and events. Not this morning. Today, she had frog-marched the children out of the house and down the street. Barely a word had passed between them. Lizzy had been struggling to keep up.

"Mummy, you're going too fast! Slow down."

"We can't slow down, Lizzy, it's important."

She was being hard. She had no choice. It was 8.45am. In just over two hours, the removal van would arrive. Ready to end one chapter of her life and start another. There was less than half a mile between their old home and their new one. It might as well have been a million.

Despite the fact she had been packing for weeks, the house didn't seem to look any different. Books were still on shelves, clothes in wardrobes. She couldn't understand how she had managed to accumulate so much stuff in a small two up, two down. Sally waited until she saw Jack follow Lizzy through the school door. Then she turned on her heels and ran back home.

She walked through the front door of the house where her life had changed forever, for one of the very last times. She surveyed the scene. She hadn't even started on the kitchen. Everything was where it had always been. Tea towels in the drawers. A dishcloth in the sink. Crockery and utensils in the cupboards. Her eyes were drawn to the window.

The shed! She had completely forgotten about the shed! She felt as though she were in one of those dreams where however fast you run, you stay exactly where you are.

Ten people couldn't get it all sorted in time. And there was only one of her. Why had she not reached out for help? Being proud didn't get you anywhere. Her mum and Rachel had offered to come round. Then the moving date had changed and neither of them could make it. She had felt awkward asking anyone else.

They had been in this house for only a few years. She still hadn't made many friends nearby. Not friends to whom she could say 'I know you're really busy but

I'm not coping'. Not friends who would listen to her funny stories about possessions that keep on multiplying and hear them as the cry for help they were. She wasn't going to ask Damien. Not if it killed her. And it might.

Sally started throwing everything into the nearest box, sealing it up and moving onto the next one. It would be a nightmare finding what she needed in the new house, but she couldn't worry about that now.

"Removals!"

Already?!

Sally could see the silhouette of a tall, wide man through the glass in the front door. She opened it hesitantly. What should she say?

"I'm really sorry. I'm not quite ready."

The man frowned. He was in his fifties and overweight for someone in his line of work. He didn't look the sympathetic sort.

"We're on a tight deadline. Footie's on later."

He walked past Sally into the house and poked his head into the living room. Packing clutter was all over the sofa and the dining table. He shook his head and tutted loudly.

"Well This is no good. I'll have to ring the boss if we can't get this sorted."

"Come on Gary, give the lady a break. At least it means we can have a cup of tea."

A second man had followed the first into the house and was now standing in the kitchen. He was wearing the same black T -shirt and blue overalls but his face looked altogether different. He turned towards the kettle.

185

"I'll make us a cuppa," he said kindly to Sally. "You carry on."

"I'm not packing, Dave. That's not our job." the fat, grumpy one muttered to his slimmer, friendlier colleague as Sally started up the stairs.

By the time they had finished their tea the bedrooms and bathroom were done. Everything was now either in a box or a bulging bin bag. Downstairs Sally picked up two black sacks from the hallway and carried them outside. As she went through the porch something caught against the plastic, splitting a bag. Empty jars, baked bin tins and wine bottles scattered all over the drive. Sally leant on her car and wept.

She had to pull herself together. There was no choice but to keep going until this was over. A new start would be worth more than a few tears and a bit of broken glass.

As she started to pick up the scattered items, the friendlier removal man came out of the house to help her. It must have been obvious that she'd been crying but he acted as though he hadn't noticed.

"Who says you have to be ready when we arrive? I like surprises," he said.

"I'll pack up your kitchen. You finish the living room. Gary can put the sealed boxes in the van. He can manage on his own. Might help him lose a few pounds."

"Thank you," said Sally. "Thank you… Dave."

She decided not to mention the shed just yet.

***

Sally was lying face down on a treatment table. She had been led through a maze of corridors to get there. Then she had been left alone. If there was a fire here right now, she was not sure she would be able to find her way out of the building.

Following the instructions posted on the wall, Sally had taken off her complimentary dressing gown and underwear. She had then replaced her own pants with paper ones. She had made a special effort to put on a decent, frilly pair today. These felt like she was wearing the 'tracing paper' toilet tissue she'd had to use at primary school.

The room was warm. The curtains were closed. Soft lamps were glowing on the dark purple walls. Music that you only ever heard in a treatment room or a Tibetan monastery was playing in the background. Sally felt herself drifting off to sleep.

"Ouch!"

The therapist had returned. She was reaching for something Sally couldn't see close to the bed. This time, Sally smelt the hot wax before she felt it being pasted onto her legs. She wasn't sure if the pain was worth it. She normally only shaved her legs a few times in the summer. If they were going to be on show. And that was in the bath with a blunt razor.

Her torturer remained silent. Sally winced at the removal of each and every one of her hairs from her ankles up to her the top of her thighs.

"Turn over please."

Sally did as she was told. At least she wasn't paying this woman who was working in the same silent and merciless fashion on the front of Sally's legs. Then it stopped. The therapist seemed to be focusing on the paper pants. Sally wondered if she had put them on the wrong way round.

"It really has been a long time, hasn't it!?"

Sally had no idea her prize would include such insights. The therapist walked over to a nearby cupboard and pulled out some super-size waxing strips.

"I'm not sure this will come with the package."

Sally was relieved when the treatment was over. She and the therapist did not utter another word to each other, even as they made their way back. When they parted, Sally watched her walk to the reception desk and lean towards a woman sitting at a computer.

"Never let me turn into THAT kind of single mum!"

Lone parenting was a club that seemed to have members everywhere. A bit like the Masons but without the funny handshake and, it now seemed, not always as friendly.

Behind the curtains of their private space, Josie was already in the hot tub. Rachel was reclining on a wicker chair nearby. They must both have finished their treatments by now. Sally put her costume on and joined Josie. The water bubbled up around her, soothing some parts of her body she didn't know could get that sore. She leant back and closed her eyes.

"How many men HAVE you slept with, Sally?"

"Josie!" said Rachel, "You don't ask a lady a question like that."

"Good job I'm not asking a lady then."

"Five," said Sally. It wasn't a number she wanted to hide.

"Shame about missing out on George," said Josie. "You could have slept with him and not added to your total."

"It's only ever been Karl for me," Rachel volunteered. "I can't imagine being with anyone else.

What about you, Josie?"

Sally threw a knowing look across the hot tub that was returned by Josie.

"Me? I lost count at number 36."

"You never take anything seriously," said Rachel laughing.

Josie opened her mouth just as Sally's phone lit up and vibrated on the nearby table. Sally stepped out of the hot water. She answered the call, while pulling a towel around herself.

"Mum," Lizzy sobbed. "I'm really sorry. Please can you come home?"

***

The move…

Rachel had told her about the house. She had telephoned Sally early one morning to say that men

189

were putting up a for sale sign in the garden opposite.

"Oh Sally, wouldn't it be fantastic if you lived across the road. Then you could come round all the time."

It would be great to have her good friends so close. And even better for the idea to have come from them. She was already round theirs pretty much all the time. She would have worried Karl and Rachel might think she was a pain, stalking them to their own road.

Rachel had suggested they go and view the house together, with the children. That day. It was a Saturday and Sally was free. She had always liked those properties. The price was in her range too. It was silly not to, as Rachel had pointed out.

They went that morning and fell in love with it straight away. Rachel with the south facing garden, Sally with the promise and potential of what felt like a home. Yes, it needed some cosmetic attention but that was what made it affordable. It was structurally sound. It was perfect.

There was only one moment of hesitation. Jack had already claimed the front bedroom and was peering out of the window.

"Auntie Rachel, Uncle Karl can't find his trousers."

Sally was in that room now. She moved across to the bay. Rachel and Karl had obscured any view into their home with net curtains. Obviously, even they had their limits.

She looked down at the road. A woman carrying a tray of two mugs and a packet of biscuits was talking to Dave, the removal man. Sally recognized her within moments. It was Josie, from the PTA. Sally watched her hand over the tray, give what looked like a very friendly wave and go into the house next door. From her raised position, Sally could see Dave studying Josie's porch intently, as he sipped his tea.

Sally turned as Gary struggled in with the metal bars of the bunk bed. He put them on the floor, put his hands on his hips, stretched his back and groaned.

"Where do you want the boxes? There's nothing written on any of them."

***

Sally, Josie and Rachel hurriedly got dressed. They signed out of the spa and asked the receptionist to call them a cab. Sally hadn't been able to get much sense out of Lizzy. All she'd heard between the sobs was 'boy', 'screwdriver', 'sorry'. She wished the taxi driver would go faster along the dual carriageway towards her home.

Eventually they reached Sally's house. Her front door was closed. All was quiet. She jumped out. She fished around for her keys in her bag. Josie and Rachel paid the driver behind her. She pushed open the door. She could see down the hall and into the kitchen. Where Damien and Lizzy were sitting.

Damien looked up. "Crisis over!" he shouted to Sally, looking self-satisfied.

He turned to speak to Lizzy. "I arrived home in the nick of time. I was your knight in shining armour, wasn't I?"

Sally saw that their daughter had been crying.

"What happened?"

Damien was in his element.

"It seems that Lizzy has a rather unsavoury admirer. He arrived today, only to find her sitting on the wall with Jack and Alex."

Sally was confused. Jack had been best friends with Alex for years. He was always at their house. Her home was regularly full of other people's children. Alex came so often she actually knew his name.

"And?"

"And... Lizzy and Alex were holding hands."

Damien stood up.

"This other lad decided the best option available to him was to threaten Alex with a screwdriver. I think that's when Lizzy rang you. Fortunately, it's also when I arrived. I gave him a piece of my mind and he ran off. He wasn't as tough as he was trying to make out."

Sally was now by Lizzy's side. She put her arms around her daughter's shoulders.

"Thank goodness you're all safe. Where are Jack and Alex?"

Lizzy sobbed again.

"They had a fight. Jack said Alex was *his* friend. He called him a bastard," she said.

Damien cleared his throat.

"Yes, that was a bit harder to sort out," he said. "I separated them but not before a few blows landed. Jack may have a black eye. He's in his bedroom. Alex sloped off looking very sorry for himself."

"Who was the boy with the screwdriver? Should we call the police?"

"No!" said Lizzy.

"Why not?"

"I love him!"

"Alex?"

"No! Cris!" Lizzy jumped up, knocking over her chair, and ran upstairs.

Sally wondered if she was still slightly dazed after her earlier aromatherapy session. She could make no sense of this at all. She followed Lizzy into her bedroom. Any mood enhancing benefits of her day of self-indulgence were evaporating as quickly as the essential oils.

"What on earth!" she said to her daughter. "Who's Cris? And if you 'love' him, as you claim to, why were you holding hands with Alex?"

Lizzy was lying face down on her bed. Her voice muffled through the duvet.

"He's my boyfriend. We're in love. It's my fault. I told him Alex liked me. Then when he came, I held hands with Alex. I wanted Cris to be jealous!"

"Well it would appear your plan worked. Even better than you intended. What are you playing at Lizzy? This isn't like you at all."

"You don't know what I'm like! You don't pay me any attention anymore! You're always out. I wish I hadn't entered you into that stupid competition! I hate you!"

Sally was taken aback. She was faced with two choices. Be the sensible adult and raise the conversation to a higher place. Or descend to her daughter's child-like level of discussion.

"I don't like you much right now either! Don't worry young lady. You'll be getting lots of attention from me. What kind of a boy threatens another with a screwdriver? You are not seeing him again. Ever. And you won't be seeing anyone for quite some time. You're grounded!"

Sally turned on her heels, walked out of her daughter's bedroom and into her own. She threw herself down onto the bed, mimicking Lizzy's position. How did she always manage to handle things so badly?

She heard Damien walk up the stairs, go past her bedroom and knock on Lizzy's door.

"Lizzy? Darling? Can I come in?"

A set of hinges slowly creaked open and Damien entered, shutting the door behind him as he went.

Sally took the opportunity to sneak out of her room and back downstairs. She allowed a small glass of Merlot to join the mix of cocktails she had already enjoyed that day. Cradling the glass in both hands, she considered what Lizzy had said. She used to know everything about her daughter. Now she had got herself a boyfriend without Sally noticing. And how had she missed that Alex liked Lizzy?

Jack appeared at the kitchen door. He looked flushed and a large bruise was darkening around his eye. Sally felt a pang of guilt. She had forgotten to check on him.

"What's for tea?"

"I don't know."

"You always say that."

"So do you."

Jack left as quickly as he had arrived. She would talk to him later. Engaging with him while he was hungry would serve neither of them well. And she had been reassured by his participation in their nightly ritual.

What WAS for tea? It would need to be quicker and simpler than ever. And something Jack and Lizzy liked.

Sally poked her head into her American-style fridge freezer. It had been a treat to herself when they moved. It had seen better days but she loved it as much as she disliked the cooker. This white good was her friend.

There was a large cauliflower in the vegetable box. It needed to be cooked or thrown away. It was only ever sensible to buy frozen but she was always tempted by the aisles of fresh vegetables that she was sure the proper mums bought. She checked the cupboards. Success!

As she broke the cauliflower into pieces, Damien appeared. Was he going to use her earlier lack of control to score points against her? He peered over her shoulder as she washed the large white florets in the sink. He looked at the jar of cheese sauce and a bag of frozen peas on the worktop.

"Cauliflower Cheese. A family favourite, if I'm not mistaken!" he said warmly.

"How's Lizzy?" asked Sally at a slightly lower temperature.

"She'll get over it. Told her not to be so silly. Said she had to be nicer to you. And that she should come down for her tea."

"Is this where I thank you?"

Damien put the bag of frozen peas back in the fridge. He took some lettuce, tomatoes and peppers from a vegetable rack Sally had never seen before and began chopping them on her wooden board.

"I'll take it from here," he said.

Cauliflower cheese

Your shopping list:
1. One large cauliflower
2. A family jar (or carton) of cheese sauce
3. Grated cheddar cheese (to taste)

How to make it:
1. Bring a large saucepan of water to the boil, then add 1 large cauliflower, broken into pieces, and cook for 5 mins – lift out a piece to test, it should be soft.
2. Drain the cauliflower, then tip into an ovenproof dish.
3. Add the jar of heated cheese sauce
4. Cover with grated cheddar cheese
5. Put under the grill until bubbling

Serve with chips - or vegetables or salad.

Chapter Twelve

The hospital didn't look as if it had changed at all. Even the cracked paint on the signs seemed to have been frozen in time since her last day at work there. The bench Sally had often sat on to eat her lunch had welcomed her again, still the same sun trap it had always been. The autumn warmth felt good on her face as she waited for Helen.

Sally picked up her phone out of idle curiosity. There were no messages. She had some updates on Facebook. There was little of interest.

When she had looked for Jon before she'd had no success. He was there on Google images as a BBC reporter, but that was all. She tried again. Nothing. He just didn't seem to exist on social media.

She searched again for George. There were lots more pictures of him in his captain's uniform, either by himself on his ship or posing with attractive women. He really was a very good-looking man. And he was a decent bloke. She wished him luck, happiness. But, despite what Josie had said, she needed more than being his girl in this particular port.

Damien had changed his profile since she last tapped in his name. He was using a new picture. One that was a least five years old. Underneath it said: 'it's complicated' instead of 'in a relationship'. He hadn't found moving in with her and the children too complicated. And he still hadn't said how long he might be planning to stay.

"Sorry I'm late! No spaces."

Helen was very obviously pregnant now. When had that happened? Overnight? Her bump was pronounced under her top. Helen herself was glowing. Pregnancy suited her. She spotted Sally staring and rubbed her tummy proudly.

"Twenty weeks! They say this is the best bit. The months that separate feeling sick and looking like a beached whale."

"You look good. I'd say you've only reached baby seal."

Helen pretended to throw her red baby book at Sally. They walked through the hospital entrance together. Sally gestured towards the disposable cup Helen had in her hand.

"Do you want me to get rid of that coffee for you?"

Helen laughed. She held the cup up higher. There was a strange expression on her face.

"It's not coffee"

Sally was confused. Helen was enjoying herself.

"I was told they'd need a urine sample, so I held it in all day. Parking took so long I was sure I was going to wet myself. My bladder was killing me. I improvised in the public toilets."

"You mean…"

"I do indeed. You can hold it for me though, while I go to the reception desk."

Sally took the cup. It was warm. How delightful. But what are friends for if not to hold each other's wee?

Helen joined a long queue of variously rotund women, waiting to speak to a harassed looking receptionist. Coffee? There was a vending machine in the corner of the room. Sally put Helen's cup on the top of the metal box while she got out her purse. She put some money in the slot, placed a paper cup under the nozzle and pressed the appropriate image.

A brown sludge that could have been anything, poured into the cup. At the same time as the machine beeped to say it was finished, her phone pinged in her pocket. She put her drink next to Helen's sample and read the message.

Don't need the wee. Being weighed already. Might be a while. Sorry. x

She picked up both cups and turned to go back to the reception area. There had to be a bin somewhere.

"Hello Sally, what are you doing here?"

"Damien! I could ask you the same question"

"My dad's in here having a check-up. He's not been feeling too good."

"Oh dear," said Sally, surprising herself with her actual level of concern.

"I'm here with Helen, although she's disappeared right now."

"She won't need her coffee then. Great."

Damien took a cup from her hand and moved it quickly towards his lips. He tipped his head and swallowed.

"Eugh! Christ! It tastes revolting! There must be something wrong with that machine."

Damien stormed off down the corridor. She probably should have stopped that happening. Maybe revenge was best served warm.

There was one chair left in the waiting room. Sally picked up a local magazine that had been left lying on the seat. It was weeks old. She sat down and opened the pages. All her life she had felt obliged to read anything available. Someone had once asked if she read the back of tomato sauce bottles. Didn't everyone?

The burnt out Smythson hotel was the centre spread. There were pictures of the building. In flames at night and then almost derelict in the daylight. Fortunately, there was no sign of either her or George.

Helen appeared. She was starting to look flushed.

"That must have been so scary," she said.

"Nearly bumping into Jon?"

"I meant the fire. You have got it bad."

"HAD. My love life is as doomed as that hotel."

Helen pulled a face.

"Well, I love you. Come on, we've got a baby to see."

The room where they would be doing the scan was barely big enough for the three people in there.

Helen lay down and lifted her top, ready. Sally stood next to her, squashed between the wall and the bed.

The medic, sitting on a tall stool, adjusted Helen's track suit bottoms, stuffing tissue around the lowered waistband. She put sticky, blue gel on Helen's stomach and pressed down on it with a plastic stick.

"There's your baby's head," she said. "You can see its heart beating. And there's ten fingers and ten toes. I don't think we've got anything to worry about here."

Helen lifted herself up on her elbows.

"Hello baby. I can't wait till you arrive. It's going to be us against the world."

Sally craned her neck to get a better look at the black and white image that was a new life in the making

"Well," said Helen, "Us and a best friend who knows how it's done."

***

The summer rain…

Sally looked at the next week's online weather forecast again. As if she might be able to change it. Just by the number of times she clicked on their holiday destination.

Brittany in August. Surely a bit of sunshine wasn't too much to ask for? Apparently, it was.

Saturday – storms
Sunday - rain
Monday – rain

Great.

Tuesday - rain
Wednesday – rain

She read on.
Thursday – clouds
Friday - sunny

Oh good. It was improving in time for them to drive home with a dose of 'here's what you could have won'.

Nothing she could do about it now. It was all booked. The car was packed. The children had gone to bed early so they would be ready for a dawn start. She had even tidied the house, although why she always tried to leave it nice for any burglars, she wasn't sure. Rachel had been primed to feed the cats. And the children were looking forward to it. They would have to make the best of a bad job. Wasn't that her specialist subject?

This was the first time they were going on holiday without her mum and dad. It had felt like something she needed to do. To prove her adulthood. The children loved being with their grandparents and she always had a great time. But sitting in the back of their car one day she had caught sight herself in the mirror. Eagerly putting her hand up with Jack and Lizzy at the offer of an ice cream.

She woke the children before it was light. They were unusually obliging and got washed and dressed in record time. Bribed with the promise of breakfast in a motorway service station, they dutifully climbed into the car without arguing about who should sit on which side. Sally got into the driver's seat and put on her belt. She squinted up at the sky. Could she make out any rays of sunshine through the grey? Not that it mattered much. She had hundreds of miles to drive before they reached their destination.

She stopped at services halfway between home and Plymouth. She let the children have whatever they wanted. It turned out to be a big breakfast each. She bought three. If you can't beat them, join them.

The ferry port was very busy. There were multiple queues of waiting cars. Sally hesitated, unsure, before choosing what she hoped was the right one. She was glad they would soon be on the boat.

The children had slept for the first fifty miles after their two sausages, two rashers of bacon, a fried egg, a hash brown, a cooked tomato (which they didn't actually eat) mushrooms, baked beans and toast. They had woken tired and irritated and were starting to pick fights with each other. She had decided to leave them to it. She couldn't steer and scold. But she had a headache. She was tired too. Her stress levels were only just within manageable limits.

They reached a kiosk. She handed over passports and tickets to a bad tempered looking man wearing a high vis jacket. He had a tattoo sleeve down his arm, decorated with sailing ships and a lighthouse. He handed the documents back.

"Lane D," he said, without looking her way.

"Thanks," said Sally.

She would have liked to turn to someone and complain about his bedside manner. Instead, she stayed quiet and moved the car into the allocated lane. Her friends had been surprised she was prepared to drive to France. On the other side of the road. She had pretended she wasn't in the least bit concerned. Now it was about to become a reality she was less sure of herself.

The back of the ferry was already open. Cars were slowly being directed into its bowels. Sally followed the flow of vehicles onto the ramp and into the ferry. She was directed into an incredibly tight space. At last the engine was off. How were they going to get out? After a lot of squeezing and stretching they escaped the car and climbed the stairs to the main ferry deck.

A woman was handing something out to each person as they walked past. Sally couldn't quite make out what it was. It was their turn. A paper sick bag was put in her hand. Then the children were given one too. The ferry worker dispensing them saw the look of horror on Sally's face.

"It's a rough crossing today. Storm force 10. You'll probably need them.

Eating now might be a good idea in the circumstances. They might have had a big breakfast but that was behind them. In front was a stormy six-hour crossing. At the entrance to the buffet restaurant it became clear all the passengers shared Sally's logic. It took twenty minutes to get to the front of the queue. It took the children almost as long to decide what they wanted.

Once they had filled their trays and paid, there were no tables to be found. They hovered near a family who looked like they might be about to leave. Sally felt guilty for putting pressure on her fellow holidaymakers. But what else could she do?

"I need the toilet," said Jack.

"Me too," said Lizzy.

Really? Now? Sally took a deep breath.

"After lunch. Hold it in."

"I can't," said Jack. "I need to go!"

Sally and Jack were carrying three portions of pizza and chips and a weird member of the trifle family composed of cream, angel delight and jelly. Lizzy was precariously balancing three bottles of pop in her arms.

"Now, mum, now!"

She had no choice. They put their trays on a large windowsill, took a drink each and left the restaurant.

Sally followed the signs to the nearest toilets. She hated this juggling act. With someone by her side they would not have lost their lunch. And when it came to toilets and changing rooms. Well, it would have been a lot simpler if she'd been left on her own to bring up same sex children. Even easier if they'd both been girls.

"You go in the boys then Jack," she said "Lizzy and I will be in the girls. If you come out before us sit in that chair there. And DO NOT MOVE." The children knew the drill. She reinforced it just the same.

When Sally and Lizzy came out, Jack was nowhere to be seen. It was perfectly possible he was still in the toilet. But Sally had no way of knowing for sure. She could be waiting outside when he was not even in there. He could have wandered off. Or been taken.

She had to keep things in perspective.

Five minutes later she could bear it no longer. She looked around for a friendly face. A friendly male face.

She saw a man about her age with his wife and children. A classic happy family. He was sorting out the children's bags while the mum got out a packed lunch and started spreading the contents across the table. He would be her first choice. But he looked too busy to be disturbed. Then his son spoke to him. He took his hand and started walking towards Sally and Lizzy.

Sally intercepted him just before he reached the toilet door. "I'm really sorry," she said, "But my son's been a long time in there. He's eight. Would you mind seeing if he's alright?"

"Of course. What's his name?"

"Jack."

The man and his son went in. After a few minutes, they came out again.

"He's fine."

"Thank you. Did you speak to him?"

"Yes."

"What did he say?"

"What? Word for word?"

"Yes please."

"Tell my mum I'm doing a poo!"

Good men did exist.

Sally settled herself into a chair next to Lizzy. She pulled something out to read while she kept one eye on the door. As the ferry pulled away from the dock, Sally again made a silent prayer, to a god she didn't believe in, that it would not be so choppy after all. He wasn't listening.

Sally and the children sat in the front end of the boat. The seats were arranged in rows like a very wide plane. Leaning her chair back, she could only see Jack and Lizzy on either side. For that she was very grateful.

She could hear one person after another retching into their allocated sick bag. The smell was truly awful. She and the children had so far managed not to succumb. Perhaps it was because they had eaten breakfast so early and hardly touched their lunch. Their stomachs were relatively empty.

"I feel bad mummy," said Lizzy.

It had started.

"Let's go outside," said Sally. "It might be better on the deck."

The air would be fresh at least. The door was very heavy. The wind forced her back. Using all their joint force, they pushed it open and stepped out. Had there been some kind of time warp? It was August. It felt like December. Only a few other people were out there. All wrapped up in big coats and long trousers. Sally and the children went to the edge of the boat. They looked over the railings. Lizzy was a strange shade of green.

"All passengers are asked to return to the inside decks. There is a risk of hypothermia outside," said a booming voice over the loudspeakers. Sally thought longingly of the holidays with her mum and dad. In a caravan in Devon. They returned to their seats, as instructed. Except Lizzy. She lay on the floor, holding her stomach.

"It makes me feel better, mummy."

Just then someone walked past with a tray of drinks. They didn't see Lizzy's legs poking out from between the seats. Hot coffee and cold lemonade flew towards her. She shouted, jumping up quickly and running to her mum. How was a trip to Brittany turning into a holiday from hell?

Two hours later they could see the French coastline through the misted windows. Soon this would all be over. Despite the odds they had managed not to throw up. Yet. It just remained to get off the ferry, drive to the motel she had booked nearby and go to bed. Tomorrow would be another day.

Sally had underestimated the challenge. They queued with other passengers who looked as bad as or worse than they did. The smell of sick filled the staircase. Once on the car deck they navigated their way to the car. Sally unlocked the doors. They squeezed in, just as they had squeezed out. Just a few minutes more till unloading. Except it wasn't a few minutes. It was five and then ten and then thirty. All the while, the boat was listing on the waves, the cars following suit. Sally looked at her children on the back seat. They looked like extras in The Night of the Living Dead. Indeed, Lizzy would have landed a lead role in any zombie film she chose.

Fifty-nine minutes and twenty seconds after getting back into the car, the ferry doors opened and the vehicles in front of them started moving forward. Then it was their turn. They negotiated the ramp and were soon on the highway. It was getting dark but the instructions said it would only take twenty minutes to get to the motel. They were close to food, a roof over their head, a bed.

"Mummy!" Lizzy screeched.

"No!" said Jack. "Not on me!"

"Get her a bag. Or a box!" said Sally. "Quickly!"

Jack reached down and handed Lizzy a small cardboard box. As she pulled into a side road, Sally saw too late that it was a supermarket box for cans, with holes at the bottom. Sally parked. She jumped out of the car, opened the back door and, with her arms outstretched to keep a safe distance between them, pulled Lizzy out.

There was so much of it. The sleeping bags and duvet stuffed into the foot space were covered. The back seat was covered. The back of the car's front passenger seat was covered. Jack had climbed through to the front. That had probably not escaped either.

Sally looked at Lizzy. Her little girl was standing on the pavement, splattered from head to toe in sick. Tears making the only clean streaks on her face. Sally wanted to hug her but she had to get her daughter out of those clothes first. She opened the boot. She pulled out a rucksack and, kneeling down on the pavement, rummaged around in its contents.

She found a top and trousers. She looked up at Lizzy again. It was fully dark now. They were lit only by the street lamp and the lights from the houses that had not yet closed their curtains.

Movement attracted Sally's attention to one of them. A man in his sixties was standing at his living room window. He was staring at them. Sally was sure they were indeed a spectacle but it wasn't helping. She stared right back. He didn't react. There was something menacing about him. Sally moved Lizzy behind the car. She didn't want him to see her little girl getting changed.

Then Sally started on the car. She thanked her earlier self for packing plenty of kitchen roll and bin bags. Once she had removed the worst of it, she put the bedding in bin bags too and put them back in the car. Sally and Lizzy got in. The man was still watching them as they drove out of the street and onto the main road.

At the motel, all three had a shower. Then the bedding was given a bath. It would still be soaking wet the next day. She would deal with that then. At least they would be clean. No one was hungry. They all just wanted the day to end. Sleep was the quickest way.

In the morning the car still stunk. It got worse when the bedding went back in. Drops of water started to fall from the sky. By the time they were ready to set off it was tipping it down. It continued to rain for forty miles and forty-five minutes. She was counting.

Sally turned onto a country lane. She followed it for a few minutes. At the *Camping À La Plâge* sign she took a right. As she reduced her speed, so too the rain slowed. Now, as she came to a stop outside the campsite office, the clouds started to lift. And with them her hopes.

"We're here!" She said to her dozing children.

She went into the office and was given a map of the site, the pitch for their tent circled in red marker pen.

As they drove up the narrow roads at what she hoped was eight kilometres an hour, Jack and Lizzy looked out of their windows, searching for plot 19. Sally saw it first. She opened her mouth to say so. Then she shut it again.

The marked-out spot - where they would be sleeping with just a thin layer of plastic lining and an airbed between them and the ground - was an enormous puddle.

It wasn't just wet. It was water-logged.

"19! 19!" said Jack. "There it is!"

The excitement in his voice turned to dismay when he too saw the water.

"Mum! I don't want to sleep there. Can't we have a caravan? Please?"

"I've only booked for a tent," said Sally. "It's August. It's supposed to be sunny!"

She parked the car to the side of the pitch. Jack was right. It would be madness to put a tent up on that.

"Let's go and see if they can give us another space,"

She and the children got out of the car and walked back to the office.

"Avez-vous un autre emplacement de camping?" asked Sally in the best French accent she could muster.

"Non."

"Caravan?"

"Aussi Non. Nous sommes plein."

"Chips!" said Sally to her children. "Let's go and have some chips!" Sally was still a firm believer in the healing power of hot potatoes cooked in oil and smothered in salt.

After a tray of chips and – for the children – ice cream smothered in yet more cream, they returned to their pitch. The water was still there. It had started to rain again. The wind was picking up too. Sally pulled the tent out of the car. They had no choice but to try.

She battled against the wind, struggling with poles and canvas. Lizzy tried to help but she kept losing her grip. Jack was stronger. But Sally still needed to be in two places at once. As soon as she pinned down one corner, another came loose. The internal fabric of the tent was getting wet. She kept losing the mallet. Where was it now? She saw it in Jack's hand.

"Jack! The mallet!"

Jack let go of the tent to walk over to her. The whole thing came away. It blew about ten yards until its progress was interrupted by a tree.

"Oh for God's sake! You stupid, stupid boy!"

Jack raised himself as high as he could and put his face close to his mother's.

"I'm not stupid, you're stupid. This is a stupid holiday. I hate it! I hate you!"

Instinctively, Sally raised her hand and slapped him across the cheek. Jack howled. Sally sat down on the sodden grass and started to cry. She couldn't take any more.

What had possessed her to think that going on holiday on her own with the children was a good idea? On holiday abroad? On holiday abroad in a tent?

What was she trying to prove? And who was she trying to prove it to? This obsession with recreating her own childhood had to stop. It was as though she felt the need to punish herself over and over again. For failing to provide her children with the only thing she had ever really wanted to give them. A mum AND dad at home.

When would she just congratulate herself on what she had achieved? She could make a life as good for her children as her own, she might even be able to make it better sometimes. It just couldn't be the same.

"I'm so sorry Jack. That was wrong of me. I should not have done that."

She stretched out her arms towards him. Jack stormed back to the car, opened the door and climbed inside. Lizzy who had been watching in horror, looked at Jack and then her mum, not sure who to console. Sally gathered the tent into a big ball and stuffed it back into the boot.

"Jump in." she said to Lizzy. "We'll find somewhere else."

Sally looked at the children. Both were looking down at their laps wrapped in their own worlds. These were not the kind of holiday memories she had wanted to create.

She drove out of the campsite and turned left towards the nearby town. After about a mile, houses started to pop up along the roadside. The gaps between them getting smaller and smaller. Then she saw it. A pretty little hotel with a small car park in front. She turned in and looked at the sign above the door. *Chambres Disponibles.*

Half an hour later they were in a family room. Sally and Lizzy would be sharing a double bed and Jack had an extendable sofa. They had unpacked, showered and changed. Sally had booked a table at dinner. She had planned to cook meatballs on a camping stove. Now the jars she brought would be left languishing redundant in the boot of her car. Jack had still not spoken properly to Sally. She reached out to touch his arm. He shrugged her away.

She walked over to the large sash windows. They overlooked a long back garden that ended sharply at a cliff edge. A wooden fence was all that protected people from a lethal drop. Sally felt like her own wooden fence was wobbling. She might fall at any moment. Jack came and stood next to her. For a few minutes he said nothing. Sally stayed silent too.

"You shouldn't have slapped me."

"I know."

"I won't forget it."

"I know."

Sally turned and faced her son.

"I do love you."

"I know." he said.

"I love you too."

***

"I want you to be there," said Helen.

She and Sally were in the hospital canteen. They were drinking something with a greater resemblance to coffee and sharing a scone.

"Where?"

"At the birth, of course. Although you have to promise to stay at my head."

Sally spluttered. Brown liquid came out of her nose and crumbs were spat across the table.

"Except that if I have to see that I'm not sure why I should spare you the mess of childbirth!"

Sally picked up a napkin and wiped her face.

"Sorry," she said. "I just wasn't expecting that."

"Who else am I going to ask?"

"Your mum?"

"How can I scream and swear at my mum? She'd never forgive me. And she'd cry at the sight of the baby."

"So you're asking me, because you think I'm a hard faced old cow who won't cry and can be told to piss off without making a fuss?"

"Pretty much."

"Then I accept."

Meatballs

Your Shopping List:
1. Jar(s) meatballs in tomato sauce

How to make it:
1. Empty contents into saucepan
2. Heat gently, for 4-5 minutes, stirring occasionally. (Do not allow to boil.)

Serve with spaghetti, mashed potato or rice

Chapter Thirteen

Sally looked at her toes poking out through the bubbles at the end of the bath. Damien had run the soothing hot water, laid out candles and even poured a glass of red wine. Now he was downstairs, giving her some space to relax. Even after all these years apart, he still knew what she needed at the end of a busy day.

There were magazines in a wicker basket on the floor. Normally, Sally would have completed this picture of bliss by reading one of them. Tonight, her mind was racing too fast. A man she might have been able to fall in love with had walked away. A second had not lived up to her rose-tinted memories. And a third, who she had previously disentangled herself from emotionally and financially, was back in her house, if not quite her heart.

If possession is nine tenths of the law when it comes to property, could presence be nine tenths of the rules when it comes to relationships? Jack and Lizzy would surely be delighted if she and Damien made a go of it again. Nothing he had ever done, no matter how selfish, had appeared to dim their love for him.

Maybe practical assistance was better than romance. Maybe for someone like her, this was good as it got? Or was she losing the plot? How could she even think of taking Damien back? Josie would certainly have a few strong words to say on the subject. Damien had done some terrible things she could never fully forgive. Yet he was here. Now. Behaving differently. They were parenting as a team. Would she feel bad about taking him back from Sharon? There was something about being there first. She looked down at her naked body. She couldn't find an ounce of guilt.

***

The crash…

Sally sat back from her desk and stretched. It had been a busy morning. A well-known actor appearing in a local theatre production had been taken ill and rushed to the hospital where she worked. She was handling press queries about his condition. And there had been a lot.

There was speculation it might have been a drug overdose. The fact she hadn't been told anything made it very easy not to give away any secrets. But not everyone believed her genuine ignorance.

For a couple of hours it had been full-on. Now there seemed to be a lull in activity. Her boss had taken advantage of the quieter phones and nipped out to get some sandwiches for them all.

Sally loved being busy. And then being able to stop pretty much as soon as the clock struck five. This job suited her so much better than the unpredictability of being a reporter.

And her more normal working day had meant she'd been able to find a professional childminder. Louise was great. Sally trusted her and could work worry free. She was sure the children enjoyed being with her too.

Often, she would see the childminder's husband. He was retired and seemed to spend every hour of the day restoring a beautiful old car. That morning he had been standing very proudly on his drive. As if waiting for Sally and the children to arrive.

"It's finally finished!" he said. "Do you like it? I might take it out for a spin later."

He'd told her what it was. A Triumph Classic? She couldn't quite remember. She had smiled and said something about how shiny its white paint looked. Then she'd pushed the children through the door and raced off in her own modern vehicle.

Sally was startled by the office phone ringing again. She'd hoped for more than a couple of minutes respite.

"Second City Hospital Press Office," she said, in as cheerful a voice as she could manage.

"Hello, It's Look Midlands here."

"I think we already spoke to one of your journalists," said Sally.

"About Peter Etherington? Yes, probably, thanks. I'm not ringing about him. There's been an accident. Some kind of vintage car, several kids involved. The ambulance is heading your way. Wondered if it had arrived yet?"

"What kind of car?"

"Let me check." Sally waited, doodling on the paper in front of her.

"A Triumph Classic. White."

Sally's heart stopped. She dropped the phone, ran out of the annexe that housed the hospital's administrative offices and made her way as quickly as she could towards its main building.

She arrived just as an ambulance was pulling in. The paramedics opened the back doors. Louise's two children climbed out, confirming her fears. Where were Jack and Lizzy? She had never truly understood the expression 'heart in your mouth'. Until now.

Then Louise stepped out too. Lizzy was in her arms and she was holding Jack by the hand. Sally rushed forward. Her children saw her immediately. They pulled away from Louise and flew into their mother's arms. The tightness by which they were holding her reassured Sally that they were unhurt.

One of the paramedics was guiding a limping Louise into a wheelchair. Sally walked over to them.

"Jack and Lizzy's Mum?" the paramedic guessed. "They said you would be here. They all seem to be fine. Just checking them out properly and then they can hopefully go home."

Sally waited with Jack and Lizzy while they were checked by the doctor. Jack was excitedly telling her how the police had arrived with sirens blaring. As though he had enjoyed the whole experience. It might have been shock of course. She would have to watch them both closely.

An hour or so later, she walked with the children back to her office to get her bag. She had rung to explain her sudden absence and her boss had given her the afternoon off. She'd even brought over sandwiches for her and the kids.

"Sorry about that," she said to the office in general. Her colleagues all smiled and made encouraging noises.

"I hope that journalist didn't think I was too strange," said Sally.

The new apprentice spoke up from the corner of the room.

"He was fine about it," she said. "He called back and I explained. He said to say he was sorry if he scared you. Jon somebody. I didn't get his surname."

***

Sally slowly made her way down the stairs and into the dining room. Something smelled good. The room looked different. It took Sally a moment to work out what it was. Damien had altered the lighting. It was dimmer, softer.

The table was laid as though in a boutique restaurant. A small bunch of daffodils was in a vase. Next to it was a lit candle and a bottle of champagne. Sally had seen this kind of romantic display in countless films and movies. No one had ever done it for her before.

Her cynical self was now losing out to the romantic one. Her head needed to work harder if it was going to outwit a heart that now might be more easily swayed.

Damien walked in. He was wearing a smart patterned shirt. She had always liked it when he made an effort. It was very similar to the ones she used to buy him. He'd teamed it with a brand new pair of black jeans. They showed off the good figure she knew he still worked hard to maintain. As he brushed past her, his scent reminded her of times long gone.

"What's the occasion?" she said. The cynic was making a dying last stand.

"Don't you know?" said Damien. "It would have been our 18th wedding anniversary today."

Sally had forgotten. She hadn't marked it since he left. Why would she? It had all felt such a deceit when it had ended so soon. Now, inexplicably, she felt guilty for that lapse of memory.

But Damien was the one who had walked away from their marriage, their family, after barely four years as man and wife. There was only one person in the room who had been wronged. It was appropriate that the last anniversary they had shared was fruit and flowers. Beautiful to look at when ripe and in full bloom, then rotten and ugly when left unattended.

"Where are the children?"

"I've bribed them to disappear. They're both on a sleepover. I wanted to say thank you. It's felt good us both being here with the kids these last few weeks."

Sally's head was buzzing. She needed to sit down. As if sensing this, Damien pulled out the dining room chair and she lowered herself onto it. She looked at her pyjama bottoms. She was not dressed for the occasion. Damien popped open the champagne. He poured her a glass. Flustered and thirsty after her hot bath, she gulped it back. He poured her another before disappearing out of the room.

Sally sat at the table. Waiting. He returned a few minutes later with something draped over his arm. It was the same colour blue as a dress she had admired when out shopping with Lizzy. It had stayed in the window display. When was she ever going to wear something like that? Damien held it up on its hanger.

"Lizzy said you liked it. She looked in your wardrobe to check your dress size."

It was beautiful. And she'd seen the price. She took it from Damien. What was the harm in putting it on when he'd made such an effort?

"Take your champagne up with you," he said, handing her the glass.

She returned to her room, took off her pyjamas and pulled the dress over her head. There was a lot of cleavage. She felt brave. She straightened her hair and made up her face, choosing the bright red lipstick she saved for special occasions. She hoped she looked as good as she felt. She took another sip of the champagne. She could feel the warmth of the alcohol coursing through her veins.

She pulled the high heeled shoes she had worn on that night with George out from under the bed. She had promised herself she would never wear them again. They hurt way too much.

As she walked into the dining room, three inches taller, Damien came out of the kitchen. He was holding two plates of Chilli Con Carne.

"You look amazing," he said.

Sally brushed his arm fondly. They took their places at the dining table She was enjoying his company. It felt like when they first met. Before it all started going wrong.

Damien took hold of her hand.

"Do you think, maybe, we could give this - us - another go?" he said.

"You hurt me Damien," she said. "You didn't just break my heart. You broke my mind."

"I know. I'm sorry. I want to mend you. All of you."

Sally's resistance was melting away.

"I can't go back there."

Damien took hold of her other hand and pulled her closer.

"I don't want to go back," he said. "I want to go forward. Into something new. It'll be different this time."

The doorbell rang.

"Ignore it." That darkness flashed across Damien's eyes. It was gone so quickly. Had she imagined it?

It rang again. Whoever it was held the button down this time. They were not going away.

"If that's Jack!" Damien said. His tone was harsh. His face seemed to harden simultaneously. "I gave him twenty bloody quid. He promised me!"

He was in the hall in moments. Sally didn't move. She listened as the front door was opened.

"Karl!"

"You bastard!"

Sally heard the sound of bone cracking bone. Then Damien crying out in pain and surprise. She jumped up, kicking off her shoes. She arrived in the hallway just in time to see her ex-husband hit the wall with his head, holding his bloodied nose as he crumpled to the floor.

***

The intervention…

Sally could not remember why she had ever supposed guinea pigs were a good idea. Well that was not strictly true. She knew why she had believed they were a better idea than rabbits. But how she had been nearly persuaded to get rabbits escaped her.

They already had two cats. Surely that should have been enough for any household. Never mind a single parent one. She was already outnumbered twice over. But no. They had moved into their new house. She had taken one look at the garden's green lawn and decided that rabbits would be great for Jack and Lizzy.

When they had gone into the pet shop, Sally had been unexpectedly gripped by panic. Rabbits got so much bigger. Two rabbits would need a lot of room. But she had promised. She couldn't back out now. Then she saw them. Guinea pigs. Like rabbits. Only smaller and with shorter ears. They would do. After some persuasion, they had returned home with two guinea pigs and all the necessary equipment stuffed into the car boot.

Now, just six months later, she opened the door to the shed. Inside were six cages - and twenty guinea pigs. The pet shop had promised that her live purchases were both male. Events had proven that they had only been right about one of them. And however much she tried to separate the new arrivals, or give them away, they kept on multiplying. Whoever coined the phrase 'breeding like rabbits' had the wrong mammal in mind.

The children had been amused at first. And then bored. Now, she alone, was cleaner, cook and nursery maid. She had been left holding the babies again. But this time it was all of her own making.

She pulled on her gardening gloves and reached into a hutch. She moved its four occupants into the purpose built run she had installed in the garden. Then she took a spade and started cleaning out the mucky straw. She craned her neck to place her head into the empty cage. She was scraping out a particularly awkward blob of guinea pig poo.

"Knock knock. Anyone in?"

Sally turned too fast, leaving behind strands of her own hair in the wire mesh at the front of the hutch.

Josie was standing outside the shed with four strong cardboard boxes at her feet. Each had air holes poked in the top and sides.

"I'm staging an intervention."

The spade was taken out of Sally's hand.

"They're all coming with me. No arguments. I can't watch this furry manifestation of a nervous breakdown any longer," said Josie.

"Think of me as guinea pig social services. They are going where they'll be properly cared for."

Sally was torn between sheer delight at the idea of seeing them go and horror at the idea that they might turn up on the table of a less fussy eatery. Did Birmingham have a Peruvian?

"Where are you taking them?" she asked.

"I have secured beds for them back at the local pet shop," said Josie. "Delightful little children will each take one and love them until they go to the guinea pig hutch in the sky."

Sally decided she was happy to accept this story of guinea pig bliss without asking any more questions. She wanted her life back. Such as it was.

***

"It was him all along!" said Karl. Throwing a punch had clearly done nothing to stem his anger.

He turned and walked back across the road. From where she was, Sally could just make out Rachel, standing in her front garden, holding the twins so tightly it looked as if their lives depended on it.

Sally looked back at Damien on the floor.

"What's going on? What have you done?"

"I haven't done anything!" said Damien, getting to his feet. Blood was running down his chin and staining his new shirt. "I get hit and you're blaming me! Get me a tissue will you!"

It was as if one man had fallen onto the carpet and another had got up from it. Sally remembered this one just as well as the other. He had arrived towards the end of their marriage and she hadn't liked him at all.

She went into the downstairs toilet and grabbed a roll of paper. She threw it towards Damien and started to make her way out of the house. She had to find out what was going on. If Damien wouldn't tell her then Rachel would.

She stepped into her open porch, looking down quickly to slip on more sensible shoes. Before she had chance to look up again, someone barged past her into the house.

"Sharon! What?" Damien was holding his hand over his nose, the tissue turning red.

"I hope that really hurts. You've had this coming for such a long time. I would have done it myself if I had the guts."

Sally could take it no more.

"Will someone please tell me what's happening!"

"He's cheated on me!" said Sharon. "Then I find out he's staying HERE!"

"I let Damien stay because he's the children's father," said Sally. "There's nothing going on between us." Sally was now sure there never would be.

"I'm not talking about you! Why would you think I mean you?"

Sharon glared at Sally. She pointed at Damien.

"He's the father of those beloved twins!"

Chilli Con Carne

Your Shopping List:
1. Jar of Chilli Con Carne Sauce
2. 300g of lean minced beef

How to make it:
1. Brown the mince in a little oil for 3-4 minutes
2. Add the contents of the jar
3. Stir and cook for at least 4-5 minutes, until the mince is cooked through.

Serve with microwaveable rice

Chapter Fourteen

Sharon was spitting her words out now. "Your friends' daughter, Laura. And him."

Damien? The father of Laura's babies? He was old enough to be *her* father. Had Sharon lost her mind?

Damien's words proved she hadn't.

"She was 18, it was perfectly legal. She told me she was being careful." He spoke in a small voice as if he was the victim, hoping he might get some sympathy.

"It's you who needs to be careful now," said Sharon. "We're finished. I'm going to ruin you. And whatever pittance you have left you'll have to spend on maintenance for four children."

"Sharon, please." Now he was starting to whine.

"Don't bother," said Sharon. "I knew you'd cheated on me. You just wouldn't admit it would you? Men! You're all bastards. Every one of you. You just can't help yourselves."

"I just wanted to see them. Laura wouldn't let me. She threatened a scene."

Sally steadied herself against the wall. So that was why he had come back. Not for Jack and Lizzy. Not for her. Not even because he just needed a roof over his head. He was using his old family to spy on

232

his new one. Family? What did that even mean to a man like him?

Damien was distracted by a buzzing coming from the pocket of his jeans. He pulled out his phone, touched the screen and put it to his ear.

"Hello?" he said weakly.

He stood up straight.

"Yes, I'm his son. Damien. Yes. Is he ok? Where are you taking him? Yes, of course. I'm coming now."

He wiped the blood off his face with more of the tissue Sally had given him.

"My dad's had a stroke. He's in the hospital. I've got to go."

Damien ran out of the door. He jumped in his car. It screeched in protest as he pulled out of the drive in the wrong gear, forgetting to turn on the headlights.

Sally had taken in the news that Ed, Damien's father, was ill. She was shocked that Laura's secret boyfriend had turned out to be Damien. The woman she had most loved to hate was standing in her hall. But her mind could only process one thing at a time. And it was none of the above. It was that she was free.

Damien had shown his true colours once more. And this time she found she *really* didn't care. She saw with brilliant clarity how badly his actions had affected her in the past, how she had quietly healed herself, how she had then tried to put things right in completely the wrong way, for completely the wrong reasons.

Things would be different now. She was once again – or was it for the first time ever - comfortable in her own skin.

A huge weight had been lifted from her shoulders. She no felt longer constrained by what society thought of her or her actions. She did not need to be with, or without, a man in order to prove anything to anyone. She did not need to be someone who did or did not have sex on a regular basis. She could just 'be'.

A year after she had given birth to Jack, she had been moving boxes of unwanted baby items to the attic room. For the first time since her caesarean she could stretch, lift and pull, just as she had before. She had not been truly aware how badly the surgery had affected her, nor had she noticed she was getting better, until she returned to herself.

Sally looked at Sharon. The two women had not been in the same room since Jack's third birthday party. The cat who got the cream had discovered it had a sell by date. She was not her rival, she never had been. All Sally's misplaced hostility towards this 'other woman' disappeared. Sharon had never promised Sally or the children anything. They had both been victims of Damien's dishonest charms.

"Do you want a coffee?"

"Have you got anything stronger?"

Sally poured herself and Sharon some of the champagne that was still sitting on the table. A relic from a lifetime ago.

Sharon drank it back. "He told me he didn't want any more children. He said that Jack and Lizzy were enough," she said.

"I don't think the twins were planned," said Sally.

"I'm sorry Sally, for what I put you through. I had no idea it felt like this. It all seemed so right. Like a force beyond my control. The real truth is, I didn't even think about you and the kids. Just what I wanted. I suppose you think I deserve this now. Well, just so you know, I kind of agree with you."

Sally took a deep breath.

"I've been wanting this to happen to you ever since you walked out of that play barn with Damien. I assumed your pain would stop mine. Now it's actually happened I don't feel anything at all. Towards either of you. I've made a good life for myself and the children. You've wasted fifteen years of yours on a serial adulterer. He will never be happy with what he has. I feel sorry for you Sharon. I won't ever be your friend again but I don't hate you."

Sharon nodded. "I better go." She grabbed her bag and walked out of the front door.

It was dark outside. It must be getting late. An image of Ed flashed through Sally's mind. She needed to tell the children about their grandad. And their dad.

***

The loss…

"I'M sitting in the front."

"No, I am!"

"No way!"

Sally pushed herself between her children who were jostling for position by the locked passenger door.

"Neither of you are sitting in the front. If you behave like babies, I'll treat you like babies. Get in the back. NOW."

They clambered in. Sally started to move the car off the drive.

"Ow!! Mum! He slapped me."

Sally was at the end of her tether. She had worked till five. Rushed home to pick up the children for their swimming lessons. Quickly got changed. She had not eaten since lunchtime and there was no chance of anything for another two hours. She pulled back onto the drive, switched off the engine and turned to her children. When she had finished talking, (screaming?), Jack and Lizzy sat in stunned silence. She turned the key in the ignition and reversed. Something black dashed out from underneath the wheels.

She looked again. There was nothing there. She must have imagined it. She continued up their street and towards the main road. Her brain would not let go of what she had seen.

"I've forgotten the towels," she said. "I just need to go back."

Jack and Lizzy stayed quiet. Their bulging swimming bags squashed between them.

Sally drove back towards the house. She scanned the drive. Nothing. Such a relief. Then she saw it. Black and lifeless in front of a house on the other side of the road.

She jumped out of the car and ran to the ball of fur. It was Fizz. She had killed her own cat.

***

As usual, Lizzy did not answer her mobile phone. Sally called Jack. The same lack of response. She waited. As usual, her phone sprang into life. She told her daughter about Ed. She would break the news about Damien face-to-face. Lizzy insisted on returning immediately from her sleepover. Sally wanted her home. As usual, Jack didn't ring back.

"It's ok mum," said Lizzy. "He's at Charlie's. I know his sister. I'll use Facebook. She'll tell him to call."

Lizzy got out her phone and started typing at high speed. Minutes later, her face fell.

"Jack's not there. Charlie's on a school trip."

Now Sally *was* worried. She tried Jack's number again. This time, it was switched off.

"I want to go and look for him," she said to Lizzy. "I can't drive. I need to ask Josie. Do you want to stay here or come with us?"

"I want to come. I can help."

As Sally walked down the drive, she noticed the shoes she had hurriedly put on in the porch hours before didn't match. Worse, she was still wearing her revealing new dress. She pulled an old fleece out of her car boot and put it on, over the top.

She knocked on her friend's door. Please let her not have gone to bed. When Josie answered it was clear she had not heard the street's big news.

"Hello! Everything ok?"

"No, not really. Jack's gone missing. I need to go and look for him. But I've had a drink."

Josie was already picking up her car keys and closing the door behind her.

"Well you've picked a rare night when I'm stone cold sober," she said, unlocking her red Renault with the remote. She didn't say anything about Sally's attire. Good friends only ever asked the right questions.

"Thank you!" said Sally, seating herself in the front. Lizzy climbed into the back. Josie pulled away, then stopped, with the car pointing towards the edge of the road, unsure which way to turn.

"Go left. Left." Lizzy spoke with increasing confidence. "He might be at the skate park."

Josie straightened the car and headed in the direction Lizzy had suggested. It was a relief that Josie did not try to chat. Surely Jack would have answered his phone if he was at the park? But they had to start somewhere. Maybe he had fallen off his bike or had got into a fight?

"Shall we call Dad?" asked Lizzy.

"He'll be with your grandad at the hospital. I don't want to bother him yet. I'm sure he'll call you soon."

"I'll call him. He won't mind."

"No!"

Sally could not risk Damien mentioning what had happened at the house.

Josie pulled up to the kerb next to the ramps and slopes used by skaters and cyclists. There were just two flickering streetlights illuminating the park. It was much more menacing at night. Sally didn't much like the look of the young people who were hanging around there either. She hesitated.

"Come on Mum. I know that boy over there. He's in Jack's year."

Sally and Lizzy got out of the car. Lizzy strode ahead. Sally had no choice but to follow her. The boy Lizzy had pointed out was sitting on a bench. He was smoking something that had a very distinctive smell. Sally wasn't that naïve. He had a can of cider in his hand. She could barely make out his face under his hoodie. He looked much older than Jack but it was so hard to tell. She didn't recognise him as anyone her son had brought home.

The boy didn't seem fazed by a woman in a cocktail dress, mismatched pumps and a fleece, accompanied by a teenage girl with a coat over her pyjamas, approaching him late at night.

Lizzy took the lead. "Hi Paul, do you know where Jack is?"

"No." The boy turned away. He clearly felt the

conversation should come to an end now he had answered the question. A girl sitting next to him in a tight t-shirt and leggings sniggered. Lizzy's confidence visibly reduced. Sally stepped in.

"We're trying to find him. Have you seen him since school?"

"Yeah. We hung out for a bit. He said he was going home to get his bike. But he didn't come back."

Sally didn't know what to make of this new information. Jack had not come home. She had been there the whole time.

"How long ago was this?"

"I don't know. I'm not his mum."

Sally was running out of patience. "Well I AM and I need to find him. He's not in trouble. His grandad's poorly."

The boy looked up for the first time. "It was after we had chips and played in the arcade. His dad had given him some money. He said he was supposed to stay away."

"Was it still light when he went?"

"Dunno. Getting dark I think."

If this boy was telling the truth, and he had no reason to lie, that placed Jack near the house just as Karl punched Damien. How much had he seen? Heard?

"He might be at Ian's house." So, the girl did have a voice then.

Ian was a friend of Jack's since Primary School. He lived nearby.

"Thank you." Sally turned to Lizzy. "Let's go."

***

The treat…

"Careful!"

Sally grabbed onto both the ladder and Jack's wobbling leg. While she was in the hall, he had climbed right to the top and was attaching a plastic skeleton to the ceiling. They all loved Halloween. Ever since Jack and Lizzy were little, Sally had over decorated the house and invited their friends for a 'scary supper'. Sally enjoyed it as much as they did. Possibly more.

This year they had focussed on skeletons, cobwebs and blood coloured window dressings. Tea was going to be spooky sandwiches followed by chocolate fingers in green jelly and red blancmange.

Sally had wondered if the children were getting too old. She had asked them if they wanted to tone it down or not bother at all. They had insisted they mark the event the same way they always had. When Sally had pointed out that she had done all the work the year before, they promised to help this time.

For once, they had been true to their word. Lizzy was in the hall at that very moment, taking down a picture and swapping it with a ghostly talking head that shrieked every time you walked past it.

They wouldn't be trick or treating this year. Their classmates were coming round to watch a horror movie. It was a school night so they wouldn't be staying over. Sally had bought lots of sweets. She wasn't sure how appreciative their parents would be of her efforts to pump their bodies full of additives and adrenaline.

241

Lizzy walked into the room. "That looks good," she said. "Well done Jack."

Jack seemed taken aback by her praise. He started making his way down the ladder grunting something that sally thought she could just make out as a thank you.

Lizzy hugged him. He wriggled away, embarrassed. "This is the best time of year," she said. "All my friends like the summer. I like it when it gets cold and dark and we have Halloween, my birthday, Christmas. It feels warm and cosy."

Right at that moment, Sally felt warm and cosy too. She had everything she wanted.

***

Lizzy needed to be told about her dad. And it was only fair to let Josie understand the series of events that had led to her driving around Birmingham in the middle of the night.

"Lizzy, there's something you should know," she said. "It might be why Jack hasn't come home."

"What?" said Lizzy, nervously.

Sally didn't know how to say it. After so many lies, the plain truth seemed the best option.

"Your dad has been having an affair with Laura. And he's the father of the twins. Karl found out today and punched him. Sharon knows too. She says she'll never have him back."

She took a breath. She made the decision as she said it, "And I'm going to tell him he has to move out of our house tonight."

Even in the dark, through the rear view mirror, Lizzy's face visibly whitened. Then she started sobbing. Small breaths at first, then big huge crescendos. Sally reached out and held her daughter's hand. Josie was trying and failing to hide her reaction to what she had just heard. Her face looked like one of those cartoon drawings, where the mouth is replaced with a letter 'O'.

Following Sally's directions, Josie found the house. Sally had never been inside. Jack always insisted he be dropped off and picked up at the kerb. This time, Lizzy stayed in her seat. Sally rang the doorbell. A woman she assumed to be Ian's step mum answered. She was in a dressing gown and slippers that didn't quite fit and smoking a cigarette.

"I'm sorry to disturb you. I'm trying to find Jack. Is he here?"

The woman looked Sally up and down. Then answered by shouting Ian's name back into the house.

There was no answer.

"They're not here." She said tersely. "They'll be fine. They're big boys."

"They're 16," said Sally. "And it's not like Jack not to answer his phone for so long."

"Sorry. Can't help you." The woman started to close the door. Sally surprised herself by pushing out her hand and stopping it.

"I need to find him," she said. "It's important."

A tall, older boy appeared behind his mother.

"Ian's with his girlfriend. I took him there. They're not together. Jack might be at the airport though. They go there sometimes."

"Thank you." Sally turned back to the car again. She checked her watch. It was already midnight. Then she checked her phone again. Nothing. She texted *Call me now!* then called Jack again.

The airport was a good fifteen minutes away. Even at this late hour the road was busy with cars whose passengers were most likely heading to or from a late-night flight. They parked in the short stay, drop off, car park. Please let Jack be here. She put a pound coin in the machine praying that before the allotted twenty minutes was up, they would be driving away with both her children.

"Do you want to come this time?" she asked Josie.

"If it'll help."

They walked across the small one lane zebra crossing and into the departures area. They scanned the large open space. There were several small huddles of people standing with their suitcases. Further in the distance a queue was forming as people checked themselves into what in her newspaper days she called a red eye; jetting off to somewhere hot. She watched their luggage being handed over and disappearing out of sight.

Where was Jack? When had he started telling lies and hanging out with boys who were drinking and worse? The knot in her stomach was now starting to feel like a rock. Its weight pulling at her heart.

There was an escalator on the right, up to the public cafes and bars. They took it in silence. When they got to the top Sally looked around again. Still no sign of her son.

"There he is!" shouted Lizzy. She ran off towards an almost empty airport bar. Sally scanned the few faces there were, none of them was Jack. Then Lizzy moved past the bar's entrance, to where the space widened out again into a large seating area with huge viewing windows.

Just one chair was occupied by a small figure dressed in black. He had his head lowered, obscured by his hoodie. Sally would know him anywhere. She breathed out for what felt like the first time in hours.

As she reached him, her relief was instantly replaced by anger.

"Jack! What are you playing at!" She shouted. "We've been looking everywhere for you! What on earth's going on?"

Jack jumped. He raised his head and faced them. He had been crying. Out of the corner of her eye, Sally saw Josie place herself at a discreet distance. Sally sat down next to Jack. Lizzy silently sandwiched him on the other side.

"Mum's been really worried," she said.

Jack turned to Sally. "I'm sorry. I wanted to be on my own. I didn't think you'd notice."

Sally felt ashamed. How could she have let Jack feel like this? She had always promised herself the children would come before anyone. Certainly any man. Even their dad. Especially their dad. Why had she let that change? Had she really become so self-obsessed?

"Why did you want to be alone?" She needed to hear Jack say it.

"I saw Karl hit dad. Laura saw it too. She told me why."

Sally hugged Jack. She did so hesitantly, unsure if he would let her put her arms around him in a public place. In any place, these days. He hugged her back. Just as tightly. Lizzy put her arms around them both. After a few moments, they released each other.

"Sharon said all men are bastards. Does that mean I am?"

"No. It doesn't. Every one of us is responsible for our own actions. And you're a good lad. I'm proud of you."

Jack attempted a smile. "I thought you and dad were going to get back together. That way you would have a boyfriend and we would be a family."

"We are a family," said Lizzy. "The three of us."

The Witch's Hand

Your shopping list:
1. Packet of green jelly
2. Packet of pink/red blancmange
3. Box of chocolate fingers

How to make:
1. Melt the jelly in hot water then leave to set
2. Add the blancmange powder to milk, heat and leave to set
3. Remove the chocolate fingers from the box

Arrange the jelly, blancmange and fingers in a grisly fashion.

Scare and enjoy!

Chapter Fifteen

Sally walked into the hospital ward. It was smaller than she'd expected. There were just four beds. Two patients on one side of the room were sitting up, talking to their visitors. A third on the other side, seemed to be asleep. None of them was Damien's father.

She looked at the fourth bed. It was empty. Next to it was a hospital armchair that had been turned towards the window. She could just make out some grey-hair, poking out from the top. It had to be him. But he didn't look like Ed. At least the back of his head didn't. And he was stooped forward. She could see that more clearly as she got closer to him.

Ed had always been a handsome man. He was in his fifties when Sally had first met him. Through her 24-year-old eyes, she could see how he attracted a string of beautiful women, so much younger than himself. Sally had pushed Damien for the introduction. He had delayed right up until they moved in together. Later he had confessed he feared Sally too might be won over by Ed's magnetic charm and good looks.

Damien's fears were completely unfounded of course. But she and Ed had got on straight away. Although she disapproved of his lifestyle, he became the perfect father-in-law. Until she and Damien split.

Then her only contact was through generous

gifts and presents for the children. Or a brief hello if they bumped into each other in town. He had simply charmed her until he didn't need her attention anymore. Just like all the other women in his life.

Damien's mother had died when he was twelve years old. Five years after she and his father had separated. She had been beautiful too. Everyone said so and old photographs proved it to be true. But she had suffered badly from anxiety and depression. Not helped by a husband who looked elsewhere for relief from her dark moods.

One incident had sparked the end of any real marriage and, Damien believed, of her life. Damien and his mother had been walking home from primary school, surrounded by other pupils and their parents, when they encountered a group of noisy office workers, spilling out of a pub and onto the pavement.

The group were very drunk. This was obvious even to seven-year-old Damien. Showing their disapproval, adults pulled their children closer and started crossing the busy road. Just as he and his mother were about to step off the kerb, Damien spotted Ed amongst the crowd. He had loudly shouted 'Daddy!', yanked himself out of her grasp and ran to his father, who was standing with his arms around the waist of a woman half his age.

Depression tightened its grip on Damien's mother. She was in and out of hospital for the next five years. Ed was in and out of their lives. Then, during one admission, she went missing. Police searched for hours before finding her body in a nearby lake. The coroner ruled it suicide.

Whenever Damien re-told the story to Sally, he alternated between feeling bitterly let down by his mother and believing she had been trying to get home to him.

Ed had not hidden how Damien cramped his single lifestyle. Until he discovered what an asset a charming teenage boy living with his widowed father could be. All that admiration, all those extra, unearned, brownie points.

Ed started bringing different women to their breakfast table most weekends. Every one of them cooing over his handsome child. He once described Damien as his 'junior partner in romantic crime'. He had clearly taught his son everything he knew.

***

The next step...

It was day one in her new job. Sally looked around the office. The signs were good so far. Although one and half hours couldn't really be a true indicator of the future. Her boss at the hospital had encouraged her to apply; a professional trade magazine placed on Sally's desk, open on the jobs page, one advert circled in heavy red pen. She wasn't sure how to react. Her boss had assured her that she needed to progress. That she would never want to stand in her way.

Sally applied to be head of communications for a new government office. And she had got the job. Now here she was. A civil servant. How had that happened? According to her teenage life map, she was supposed to be reading the News at Ten. Didn't her mother tell her that life was what happened when you were busy making other plans?

Her career might have been an accident. It could still be a happy one. She had already spoken to her team and said hello to other people whose names she would not remember. Everyone was very friendly.

But she was at a senior level now. More was expected. Less was handed to you on a plate.

She played with the new notebook and pens she had treated herself to at the weekend. It was like a first day at school. She hoped she had done the right thing. She was still ambitious. Her career meant more to her than money, however much she needed that. It gave her confidence. Provided her with a space of her own. It was something at which she could succeed. And this job was her greatest challenge so far. It would mean more hours and more demands. She would have to go to London sometimes. Her children always came first. But they were older now. Just as you were told to put your own oxygen mask on first if you were unfortunate enough to be on a plane hurtling towards the ground, she needed to look after herself in order to look after them.

A member of her new team had put a contacts list on her desk She looked through the series of organisations and telephone numbers. She would need to introduce herself to the media pretty soon. She might as well start now.

The phone answered after two rings.

"Hello, Look Midlands reporters' desk"

"Hi. It's Sally Stainton from the Second City's Government Office. I was hoping to speak to a reporter. I've just started as the head of comms and I wondered if I could invite you out to lunch, to properly introduce myself."

"Oh. Hi Sally, thanks for calling. I'll have to decline, I'm afraid. I'm about to head off on holiday. You could try Pete Knowles. He does a lot of the political stories. Although he can be a bit grumpy. Tell him Jon said to be nice."

"Thanks, I will. Jon who?"

"Sorry, my editor's shouting at me from across the office. Gotta go. Do try Pete, won't you?"

***

"Hello Ed,"

The man in the battered, hospital chair WAS her former father-in-law. An older, scruffier, version, yes, but still him. The Ed she had known for so long would be distressed at the Ed he had become.

He used to take great pride in his appearance. This Ed looked haggard and unkempt. His silver hair was greasy and unbrushed. He had a few days of white stubble on his chin. His face was off balance. One half hanging down in a way that forced his mouth open and was the cause of a gentle trickle of saliva running down his chin.

He was wearing a hospital dressing gown that hung open to reveal yet more white hairs on a saggy old man's chest. One of his arms was placed across his lap, as though it didn't quite belong to the rest of his body. Sally was glad she had come to visit during the day while Lizzy and Jack were at school. She would be able to prepare them for what they would find.

He tried to smile. It was more of a wonky grimace. He gestured with his workable right arm for Sally to sit down. She grabbed a plastic chair and placed herself in front of him.

Ed pointed to a pen and paper on the bedside table. She handed them to him. He looked at her again. She put the newspaper she'd bought for him underneath the blank sheet of paper. She was not sure it would be needed for anything else.

It took him ten minutes to write down a few short words, Sally sat by his side, mourning the vivacious, terrible, fantastic, awful, attractive man she had once known. He gingerly waved the handwritten message. Sally took it from him and looked at the huge scribble on the page. The first line was easier to make out than the last.

Damien is not a bad boy. I'm a bad dad. Bad husband.

Sorry.

She screwed up her eyes to read the rest.

I know loves gone. He needs kids. Hate me. Forgive him.

Sally had once been told that indifference was the best revenge. It was only now that she realised forgiveness was also the best medicine.

Ed looked at her. Expectantly. He appeared to be exhausted. As if he had just completed a short run not a short note. She smiled at Ed, stood up, and kissed him gently on the forehead.

"I don't hate you Ed. How could I? And if I can't hate you, how can I hate Damien? I forgive you both. You've lost so many wonderful things that were yours for the keeping."

Sally walked towards the exit. She would cook fish pie tonight. The children liked that.

Fish Pie

Your shopping list:
1. One jar of fish pie sauce
2. One 11oz mixed fish pack
3. Bag of potatoes (to mash)

How to make It:
1. Pre-heat the oven to 200^{0}C, 400^{0}F, Gas mark 6
2. Place mixed fish in an oven proof dish, pour over sauce and top with mashed potato
3. Add cheddar cheese before baking.
4. Cook for 40-45 minutes, or until the fish is cooked through and the potato is golden

Serve with peas.

Chapter Sixteen

Sally was woken by the sun streaming through the uncurtained landing window, passing through her open bedroom door and onto her bed. She was ready for a new beginning. After her first visit to Ed, she had gone again with the children. Back home, they had talked more openly than she could ever remember.

Things were still far from perfect with Jack. But they had connected as mother and son. She had discovered he did still need her. He knew she was still there for him. She could sense a change in Lizzy too. Her daughter seemed happier and more self-confident.

She had worried they both would react badly to the news of their dad and the twins. Jack had dealt with it quietly. Lizzy had accepted the idea, spending more and more time over at Rachel's. She had even chosen to write a children's story based on the twins for a GCSE project. The house felt better now Damien had gone. His presence had been an oppressive cloud that they hadn't felt until it was gone.

She threw off the duvet and looked at her body in the tatty old pyjamas she had been wearing for years. She would get some new ones. She would lose some weight too. And get her hair done. Her eyebrows. Maybe even her nails. Somewhere expensive. Why had she not bothered just because no one was looking? She wanted to feel good again. About herself. For herself.

She got out of bed and started rummaging through her wardrobe. She found some old pumps, a tatty t-shirt and some shorts. She couldn't wait until she had the proper gear. If this was the first day of the rest of her life, she didn't want to waste a moment. Dressed in her makeshift running clothes, she moved quickly down the stairs. She wrote a note telling the children she'd be back soon and opened the front door. Sunlight bounced into the hallway. It was one of those beautiful October days you forget about until they come around again.

Sally breathed in and took her first step. She had not been running since school. Her sporting abilities were on a par with her cooking. And her response had been the same. Avoiding the challenge. Hiding in the long grass or at a friend's house, to avoid sports day or cross country runs.

She moved slowly at first and then faster. Powerwalking they called it. She felt powerful. Any remaining rocks of bitterness and anxiety fell out of her emotional backpack and were discarded on the side of the road.

***

The trampoline…

As she turned the key in the door, she sensed emptiness. The absence of sound weighed down on her shoulders. Sally was in two minds about silence. Opportunities to sit quietly somewhere, with no distractions, to read a book or put her thoughts in order, were rare and valuable. But silence was not always golden. Sometimes, such as today, it brought on a sense of foreboding.

"Hello!"

Nothing. The children were old enough to make their own way home these days. But it was unusual for neither of them to be there when she returned. Something caught her eye. Down the hall and into the kitchen. Something that wasn't right.

The french doors out into the garden were open. Wide open. The sun was shining brightly into the house, lighting up a strange, big, blue, object, poking into the room. Sally moved closer. It was the children's old trampoline, pushed against the back of the house.

Sally sat at the kitchen table. Too exhausted after a day at work to investigate further. She leant down to take her shoes off. Her feet were aching. Then she noticed there were muddy footprints running through the kitchen from the trampoline. She couldn't leave it now.

She followed them. Out of the kitchen and into the hall. How had she not spotted them when she came in? They stopped at the bottom of the stairs. No, they didn't. Every second step was imprinted with at least one, dark, shoe-shaped mark.

Sally made her way up towards the landing. At the top of the stairs the footprints went straight into her bedroom. Her door was open. She always closed it when she left in the morning.

Were Jack or Lizzy in her bedroom? Hiding? Had something awful happened? There had to be an explanation. Sally moved nervously towards her room. There was no one there. The footprints carried on. They stopped at the edge of her bed. Then they started again. Over the expensive duvet cover that she'd treated herself to the month before. Back onto the carpet. And onto the windowsill. They ended there. Where else was there to go?

Sally was torn between fury at the mess that had been created and fear at what this meant. She was desperate to look out of the window. She really didn't want to look out of the window. She looked out of the window. She peered down. Fifteen feet below her was the trampoline.

It had to be Jack and his friends. This was not Lizzy's idea of fun. And Sally could not imagine a burglar taking the time. She looked around the garden for any dead or horrifically injured young boys. Jumping out of a window onto a trampoline with no netting seemed to be a fairly high-risk endeavour. She couldn't see anyone. Perhaps she ought to check in the overgrown borders.

"Hello? Mum? Lizzy?"

It was Jack coming into the house.

"Anyone want some chips?"

"You've certainly had yours!" shouted Sally as she stormed back down the stairs.

****

"I've got something to show you."

Rachel was sitting in her kitchen with Sally and Josie. It was a Saturday afternoon. They had been there for hours, drinking coffee and putting the world to rights.

"Unless it's a glass of prosecco, I'm not interested," said Josie. "Surely it must be wine o'clock by now!"

Rachel looked at her disapprovingly.

"You can have wine. I'm sure there's some in the house. But I've found something to make us healthier and fitter. Sally inspired me when I saw her jogging past the house last week."

Josie guffawed. "Don't you mean 'jalking'?"

Josie and Sally made faces at each other across the table.

"Don't be rude, Josie," said Rachel. "Sally will live longer than both of us if we don't start exercising too. I've found a running club for beginners. For women like us. 'Running Girls'."

Josie walked to Rachel's fridge and opened the door.

"Well, this girl doesn't run. You can count me out!"

"Oh, come on." said Sally. "It'll be fun."

Rachel nudged Josie out of the way and pulled out a bottle from the very back of her fridge.

"It's an eight-week course to get you feeling fitter. Couch to 5K."

Josie reached for two glasses for her and Sally.

"How many weeks do they let you stay on the

couch?"

"Well I'm going to do it," said Sally. "It's really hard running on your own and I've no idea if I'm doing it right."

Josie looked at Sally, her face saying it all, before pouring the wine. Without asking, she opened Rachel's bread bin and peered in.

"Sorry, I'm sticking with cake to Cava."

***

The last go…

The first time Sally saw her new neighbour was the day he moved in. He arrived at the house opposite hers with a car full of belongings and a dog. She was kneeling in the garden pulling up some particularly annoying weeds. This gave her the perfect opportunity to peer, unseen, through the overgrown blackberry bush.

She and Josie had noticed the house was up for rent. They had joked about the man of their dreams moving in and taking them away from 'all this'. They were never quite sure what 'all this' was that they needed to get away from. Or how he could take them away if he lived across the road. They enjoyed these fantasies all the same. The two women would play 'Boy Bingo' every time someone came to the street who looked remotely eligible. Crossing off their requirements as and when they were met. Each box always getting harder to tick.

A man?

Straight?

Single?

These three were essential. The other criteria were more flexible depending on how long it had been since they'd played.

Someone their age? (not illegal or nearly dead)

Good looking? (not ugly)

Rich? (not poor)

Interesting? (enough for one date)

It was appalling behaviour. If a man had told them he was doing it about women, they would have shaken their feminist fists at him. But it was fun. So they carried on.

Handsome, and, she guessed, in his late thirties, the stranger climbed athletically out of his car and started taking his possessions from the back seat and into the house. She forgot all about the weeds and sat back on her legs. It was rude to stare. She kept on looking.

She couldn't have said how long she'd been sitting there when the man opened the back of his car and the dog leapt out. It must have been more than a few minutes. Her joints had stiffened up. She didn't have time to move out of the way as a mountain of ginger fur bounded across the road and into her garden. The dog's tail wacked Sally across the face and sent her sprawling.

"Rusty! Rusty!"

The man was in her garden now. He grabbed his dog and walked over to Sally. She was still lying stunned on the grass.

"Are you alright? I'm so sorry. I've just moved in across the road. My dog's a bit over excited."

Sally felt a bit overexcited too.

The second time she saw her new neighbour she was at her kitchen sink. Looking out of the window. He came out of his house to put his bins on the kerb. He looked up and waved. She waved back. Then instantly regretted not taking her pink marigolds off first. How ridiculously retro did she look? She had only put them on to deal with some particularly stubborn scrambled egg at the bottom of a pan.

He was crossing the road. Coming in her direction. Up her path to the front door. She pulled off her gloves and rushed into the hall. Opening the door before he even had time to ring the bell. He put his raised arm back down by his side.

"Hi, I'm Martin. You met me and my dog last week. I hope you don't think I'm being too forward but I'm new to the area. You seem to be on your own, like me. Do you fancy going out for a drink sometime?"

Streamers and balloons filled Sally's head.

The third time she saw her new neighbour, he was standing by the bar in the pub on the corner of her street. Waiting for her to arrive for their date. They ate, they drank, they talked. Maybe Sally talked more than he did. Maybe Sally talked too much. At the end of the night he kissed her politely on the cheek and they went into their separate homes.

The fourth time was the very next morning. Early. He was packing his belongings into his car. She had got out of bed and opened the curtains. There he was. He hadn't mentioned a trip. He was clearly going away for a while. He put the dog into the back and closed the boot door. Then he started making his way to her house.

She slid down onto the floor so he wouldn't see her. She wasn't going to answer the door. Not in this state. Her 'just got out of bed' look was even worse than her 'weeding the garden' look. And that was bad enough. She waited a few minutes. The bell didn't ring. Perhaps she had been wrong about where he was heading. She dared to look again. Her phone pinged just as he drove away.

Thanks for last night. I have decided to go back to my wife.

Really? One evening with Sally was enough to persuade him to turn on his heels and go back home? What did that say about her pulling power?

Sally resigned herself to her fate. If at first you don't succeed, give up and appreciate your family and friends so much more instead.

***

Sally and Rachel were on route to their first 'Running Girls' session in the local park. Neither had got around to buying any new kit. They had though followed the suggestions on the website and brought a water bottle and a small money bag for their phones and keys.

"What possessed me to come up with this idea?" said Rachel.

"We're doing our best to live to a ripe old age," said Sally getting out of the car.

Rachel locked the doors. "But what kind of life will it be?" she whined.

The two women walked across the car park. Every vehicle they passed emptied itself of another female roughly their age, in running gear. Some had clearly spent a small fortune on the right clothes. Others, like them, were wearing tracksuits and t-shirts that had been stuffed at the bottom of a wardrobe for years.

They approached a circular, tarmacked, area, in the centre of the park. Sally and Rachel pulled out their phones and found their emailed membership forms. They showed them to the staff and waited for the session to begin. Sally had been worried that everyone else there would be fit and toned. She was relieved to see they were all shapes and sizes.

A woman in a green hoodie with 'Running Girls' written on the back climbed onto a nearby bench.

"Ladies! Ladies! If I can have your attention, please."

A mass of heads turned towards her, their voices going quiet.

"Thank you. Welcome to week one of this series. We plan to have you all achieving the Couch to 5K challenge by week eight, however ready you feel today."

The woman paused to let her words sink in.

"We believe you can do this because we've done it before. Because ladies just like you have done it before. We're not saying it's easy, and it won't come without hard work. But it's possible."

Someone shouted out from the group.

"Is it too late to back out?"

Laughter rippled across the gathered crowd. The woman standing on the bench smiled, she was clearly used to this gentle heckling.

"The good news is that you are not expected to get there in one go. Each week we will be building up your stamina, taking it gently at first, and then gradually working up to periods where you feel able to take more on. Over time, it will come naturally to you. You will be succeeding without even thinking about it. All it takes is remembering to breathe."

Sally wished she'd had this pep talk when she first became a single mum.

***

The honest broker…

"Oh Sally. You poor thing! Forget him. Forget all of them. Who needs men anyway?"

"Hopefully, you do Rachel," said Karl, grabbing another beer from the fridge. "I wasn't planning on going anywhere."

"Don't be silly Karl. You know what I mean. We're lucky."

Rachel gave Karl a peck on the cheek.

"Although I don't always feel that way when I'm picking your smelly socks off the floor."

Karl grabbed her waist.

"Love me, love my smelly socks. Wasn't that in our vows somewhere."

"Get a room will you!" Sally scolded affectionately. They were luckier than they would ever know.

Karl waved a piece of paper in the air.

"I think you'll find we live here. And I won't be told what to do by someone I have just discovered has been insuring her dead cat for the last five years."

It was Friday night and she and the children were round Rachel and Karl's again. As they had been for so many Friday nights in the past. And she hoped would be in the future. This particular evening they had come early. Karl had offered to help Sally sort out her finances.

"What!" said Rachel, grabbing Sally's handwritten budget from Karl's hands.

"Oh, Sally, what are we going to do with you?"

Her face changed as she studied it further.

"Wait a minute. What's this? A health and beauty budget? Karl! How come I don't get one of those?"

Sally had known it was time to start being honest with herself and get things back on track. She was now regretting just how honest she had been with her friends.

"I copied it from a magazine! It's only for my hair."

Her words were falling on deaf ears. You didn't need to be a former journalist to know this story had legs.

She treasured these evenings. However tired she was from a week of work and house and children, she could be in a place where she could relax. Where she could laugh at herself, eat curry, drink wine and fall asleep on the sofa. She was lucky too.

***

Sally had decided to venture beyond her normal repertoire and attempt pork in sweet and sour sauce. Still using a jar of course, she wasn't that brave. But it was a not a meal she could remember doing before.

Her mobile rang. She rubbed her hands down her apron and picked it up. Could bad vibes travel down telephone lines? She could tell it was Damien before he even started speaking.

"Hi Sally, how are you?"

"I'm good. Cooking tea," she said, warily.

Damien continued.

"Lizzy's asked me to buy her a jacket she's seen. But it's not her birthday for ages."

If only Sally could wait for birthdays before she had to buy the children new clothes.

Damien coughed. He lowered his voice as if someone had come into the room where he was talking.

"The thing is, I can't keep throwing money at her."

He had excelled himself. Sally could not allow this moment to pass.

"Well, if you've been throwing money at her Damien, you've been missing."

Sweet and Sour Pork

Your shopping list:
1. Jar of sweet and sour sauce
2. 200g long grain rice
3. 600g chopped pork
4. Chopped green beans
5. Spring onions

How to make it:
1. Boil 200g of long grain rice until done, then rinse and drain.
2. Cook 600g of chopped pork until done, add chopped green beans and spring onions and cook for a further two minutes.
3. Add sweet and sour sauce and simmer for a couple of minutes.
4. Stir in the rice and allow it to warm.

Chapter Seventeen

Sally had made it. Here she was. About to run a timed 5K. Without stopping. Could she now call herself a runner? The celebrity on her training app had told her so.

She had certainly lost weight. It must be more tomato soup and less alcohol. Well, not much less alcohol. She wasn't the living embodiment of some superstar fitness video. But at least the only person she might be lying to was herself.

The 'Running Girls' course was coming to an end. This was the finale. Doing it for real. Parkrun. What it said on the tin. Five kilometres in a park on a Saturday morning.

Everyone from the group was there. Everyone except Rachel. She had phoned minutes before they were due to leave, saying she couldn't make it. Sally had not tried to persuade her otherwise. Some kind of row was brewing in the background.

There must have been about two hundred people there. All moving to keep warm in the early December sun. They were beginning to queue up. They were crowded together at the front, then spreading out as the line snaked its way along the path behind them.

The fastest would go first. They would probably finish before she even reached the starting line. She had looked at the average run times on the internet.

The top ones were coming in at around fifteen minutes. It could take her that long to tie up the laces on her trainers.

Behind them were the keen ones, just as competitive but not quite as quick. They had probably been running all their lives. They certainly looked the part. She fought an irrational dislike of these people. They were the ones at school who had won all the trophies and captained the teams. She didn't begrudge them their prizes or their glory. However, the sense of shame at being argued over because they did NOT want her for their team had never really gone away.

Next were the 'most improved'. It didn't come naturally but they were able to hold their heads up high when they ran through the finish line. Of course, if most improved meant going from completely rubbish to really bad, then she could feature in this category too.

She knew her place though. It was at the back with the 'also rans'. They came, they ran, they (usually) finished. Who cared what time they did it in? Someone had told Sally these were the real heroes of the day. She pretended to believe it.

She looked around to find someone she might be able to keep up with, to make sure she wasn't a lonely last. It was hard to choose. Being bigger did not always make people slower. Having the right clothes did not make them faster.

Then she saw them. Right at the back. Two men who appeared to be the combined age of the rest of the long line of runners. Their elderly faces were etched with lines, showing their years, like the rings in the trunk of a tree. They were talking, their heads close together, wearing identical navy t-shirts and shorts. They had the same mop of white hair on their heads, the same long noses and friendly smiles.

A large woman in the queue turned towards Sally. "That's Bill and Ben."

Sally blushed at having been caught staring. "Bill and Ben?"

"Yes. No one knows who was here first. Them or the Flowerpot Men."

The stranger was warming to her subject.

"They're incredible. Identical twins. And it's their birthday today. Eighty! Everyone loves them. Especially those of us coming up the rear. They're so nice. And they mean we never come last."

They were who she had to beat. Two octogenarian birthday boys. Harsh. But true.

The whistle blew. The front runners disappeared in a cloud of dust. Sally walked to the cones that marked the beginning of the beginning. She picked up her feet, moved her arms backwards and forwards in time with her legs and reminded herself to breathe in and out.

They started on the flat. This wasn't too bad. She was pacing herself though. She didn't want to run out of energy halfway round. Sally got into her stride. She was almost enjoying herself.

She completed one lap in 20 minutes. She could do this. She was sure of it. There were still five people behind her; she had checked as she turned one of the corners.

The well apportioned woman who had told her about Bill and Ben went past, her enormous boobs bobbing up and down as she ran. Did Sally look as unsuited to the task at hand? At least they were trying. They were both faster than all those still in bed. Although part of her wished she was still curled up under the warm covers, another was pleased to be grabbing an early start on the day.

She was then overtaken by a small man and a tall woman she hadn't noticed before the run began. She had half a lap to go. She was confident she could make it to the end. She had to make sure she did so more quickly than the elderly twins.

A volunteer marshal appeared from between the trees at the side of the path and started collecting up the distance markers as she approached them. Really? Was that necessary? Were they going to leave the finish line in place?

At least she wasn't last!

She heard the old men behind her. The competition. They were catching up. And they were doing so whilst chatting.

"Where's he going to be?" one of them asked.

"Round the next corner. That's what he said anyway. They want to film us running before we stop and talk to him."

"Fancy us being on the telly. I hope we don't look silly."

"Well if I do, I'll say it was you."

The two identical men continued to run and talk to each other.

"What's his name again? The reporter?"

"Jon something. Oh yes, Oldman. Rather appropriate today, don't you think?"

Sally felt hot and clammy. And not from the effort of moving her legs against their will.

***

The launch…

Everything had been in place to launch a new partnership between her government department and thousands of local businesses. It wasn't the most exciting story ever to hit the headlines. But that was what had made Sally even more pleased with the attention it had started to receive.

Lots of people had worked hard to make it happen. Her team had designed graphics and social media posts. They had made a video and written a leaflet encouraging others to take part. They had sent out an embargoed press release. And the media had bitten. Not just newspapers but television too. She had earned valuable brownie points with her boss when she told him that Look Midlands had asked for a pre-launch interview.

What could possibly go wrong?

This!

The Minister who had been going to front the whole launch had been forced to resign. He had said something very rude about the Prime Minister to an off-duty reporter, who had then proved reporters are never off duty.

Now the FORMER Minister was all over the news. National and local. But not for the reasons Sally had hoped. And he had gone into hiding. After the 'obligatory' interview with journalists at his garden gate, with a tray of tea and biscuits in his hand, he and his family had been filmed getting into their car and driving off. No one had been able to get hold of him since. Well not anyone Sally knew.

Broadcast journalists were so hard to please. She still hadn't managed to meet a Look Midlands reporter. Now she had to turn one away. It would make them even less likely to take the bait next time. She nervously called the newsdesk.

"Hello, it's Sally Stainton here from the Government Office. Listen, I'm really sorry about this but we're going to have to cancel the interview with the Minister. I'm sure you'll have seen he's resigned."

"It's the talk of the newsroom. I thought you might give us a call. To be honest, even if it had gone ahead, we wouldn't have been talking to him about your scheme. Has he resurfaced yet?"

Sally didn't want to sound as ignorant of the MP's movements as she really was.

"I doubt it. Sorry. He's left the city with his family."

"Oh well. Thanks for letting me know. It was going to be my story. I might even get away early. As long as my editor doesn't give me a last minute 'And Finally'."

***

Sally stopped suddenly. The two men narrowly missed running into her, skirting around her bent body as she leant forward to get her breath.

Jon? Around the corner? She still thought about him sometimes. Wondered if she might bump into him again. Just to say hello of course. Nothing more. In her imagination it had never looked like this. SHE had never looked like this.

The men were in front now, running backwards, slowly, looking at her inquisitively.

"Are you alright dear? You look like you've seen a ghost."

Sally nodded. She did not have the energy to speak.

"Well if you're sure. It's just there's someone waiting for us."

She waved them away. She tried to smile but it was more of a scowl. The men turned to face the right way and increased their speed. One of them turned back and shouted to Sally as they disappeared from view.

"We've got cake. Come and join us."

Sally could not let this happen. They could have their cake. But she would not let Jon see her eat it.

Not all red and sweaty and being beaten by runners who had nearly two hundred years between them.

She badly wanted to complete the run. She had worked hard for this. She looked either side of her, weighing up her options. A small path, where grass had been worn away by walkers looking for a shortcut, ran through the trees and bushes to her left. She was pretty sure it joined up with the main path on the other side, just before the finish.

She took it. There was no one behind her to see what she'd done. If she was lucky no one would spot her re-joining the route. It was cheating, yes, but she was only cutting off one corner. The others were well ahead by now. She wouldn't interfere with anyone else's position. Her own time would be wrong. That was a price she was willing to pay.

The sun could not penetrate through the twigs and thorns and it grew increasingly dark as she was surrounded by more and more undergrowth. Sally ran faster. She wanted to get out of there, finish and go home. She could see a growing patch of light on the other side. She was nearly done.

She had misjudged it. She could see Jon and his camera man, Simon. They had placed themselves just where she was due to come out.

She veered off her route and into a dip. There had been a big rain storm a few days before. The path was muddier than Sally had expected. The bottom of the dip was flooded. She tried to stop herself. She had too much momentum. She slipped and fell in face first. Sally gave out an almighty shriek.

She gathered herself onto all fours. The water came up to her elbows. Every time she tried to stand, her hands and feet slipped in the mud. She manoeuvred herself into a sitting position. She was stuck and soaking wet. It couldn't get much worse.

"Sally?"

She had to stop thinking that. As always, she was wrong. It could.

Jon looked down at her from the top of the dip.

"What's a nice girl like you doing in a place like this?"

Sally had no dignity left to protect.

"Avoiding you."

"Me? Why?"

Sally's answer was news to her too.

"Because I still like you. A lot."

Jon grabbed a branch to keep himself steady. "What about your ex?"

"Damien? He's still my ex. Is that why you stayed away? I thought I'd scared you off."

Jon started laughing. "Well, you are quite scary!"

Sally was taken aback. "It's not funny!"

"Oh. I'm sorry, Sally, but it really is."

Jon smiled at her. That kind smile that had warmed her heart so much when she first met him. She took in her situation. It was as if she was looking down at herself, sitting there in the cold, muddy water, covered in dirt from head to toe. She started laughing too. And once she started, she couldn't stop.

Jon released the branch and waded into the water. She noticed he was wearing new shoes.

"Let's get you out of here," he said.
Jon offered Sally his hand. She took it and he pulled her up in one go. How strong he was. She wobbled. He put his arm around her to hold her steady. She fell in towards him. She didn't move away. He didn't let go. They turned their heads to look at each other. Their lips were so close she could feel that same charge of electricity running between them.

"May I?" said Jon.

"Yes," said Sally.

He kissed her. Sally was standing in a foot-deep puddle, with cold water running down from her hair across her face. She was so warm. It could only have lasted seconds. It felt like forever. She was exactly where she wanted to be.

There was a noise in the undergrowth. Jon broke away.

"They'll be coming to see why I'm taking so long. And we really should get you out of this water. You'll catch pneumonia."

Jon and Sally scrambled up the bank together and made their way out of the bushes. Simon was on the path at the edge of the trees.

"I was about to send a search party,"

He looked disapprovingly at Jon's soggy trousers.

"So much for the shot of you giving Parkrun a go. We won't be able to explain that."

Sally felt the need to defend him.

"I fell over. He rescued me."
Jon shook his head.
"It's Sally," he said.
"SHE rescued ME."

Tomato Soup

Your Shopping List
1. One tin tomato soup

How to make it
1. Put the soup in a saucepan
2. Heat slowly, do not boil
3. Pour into bowls

Serve with crusty bread

Starting Again…

Not for the first time, Sally was late. The disastrous, failed, launch would provide her latch key children with more opportunities to jump out of windows or spill drinks down the sofa.

The texts kept coming on her phone. 'Where was she?', 'When would she be back?', She didn't want to know why they seemed to care so much about her whereabouts this afternoon.

She looked at her watch. 3pm. It had only been 1pm a few seconds before.

Her locker fought against her attempts to open it. She heard the thud of papers falling down the back as it finally gave way. She stuffed in more documents, swearing to herself would deal with that tomorrow.

She needed a wee. Maybe if she didn't think about it she could last until she got home. She had six minutes to catch her train. It took five to get to the station.

The heat made it harder to run and she arrived with no time to spare. She could see her train from the top of the stairs, sitting at the platform, the last stragglers climbing on.

Taking two steps at a time and pulling her ticket out of her bag, she almost fell. The guard paused and smiled at her as she raced through the barrier and into the nearest carriage.

Sally was breathing hard, as though she had run a marathon. She collapsed onto a seat. She needed to stop thinking about exercise and actually do some.

The train pulled away. Her concerns about catching it disappeared, only to be replaced by a demanding bladder and worries about what she would find at her destination. She looked around for a distraction. The man next to her seemed to be enjoying himself, He wasn't worried what was waiting for him. Or whether he would wet himself before he got there.

As she got off the train and started walking, she continued to go through the various scenarios that might have played themselves out at home. She was jealous of all the happy families who shared her street. Although who knew what crosses they themselves had to bear?

It was quiet. Too quiet. She strained her eyes to see her house at the bottom of the road.

She hurried. She was almost there. She checked for cars, took a step… and stopped.

Boeuf Bourguignon*

"It's a mystery to me how this giant of the French classical repertoire has escaped the clutches of this column for so long. Richard Olney (another big beast of the Gallic cookery scene) describes boeuf bourguignon as 'probably the most widely known of all French preparations', while Elizabeth David introduces it as 'a favourite among those carefully composed, slowly cooked dishes, which are the domain of French housewives and owner-cooks of modest restaurants rather than of professional chefs'.

Sounds manageable. Yet Olney goes on, slightly worryingly, that 'beef burgundy certainly deserves its reputation – or would if the few details essential to its success were more often respected. There is nothing difficult about its preparation, but there are no shortcuts.' And David doesn't help the situation, with the airy assertion that 'such dishes do not, of course, have a rigid formula, each cook interpreting it according to her taste'.

According to Larousse Gastronomique, *la bourguignonne* refers to anything (generally 'poached eggs, meat, fish or sauteed chicken') cooked with red wine and 'usually garnished with small onions, button mushrooms and pieces of fat bacon'. That much we know. Everything else, it seems, is up for grabs."

See page 7

Chapter Eighteen

Sally was standing in the middle of the room. Somewhere so familiar. Yet feeling so strange. She was attempting something new. Something scary. Something she had avoided for so long.

She folded the newspaper down the middle and then in half again, flattening the pages. She had never paid much attention to this part of her Saturday supplement before. Occasionally she might look at the pictures and imagine a parallel universe where such images might bear some relevance to her life. Then she would turn to the family pages full of domestic trials and tribulations that she could identify with so much more easily.

She looked at the fixture dominating the room. It stared back, daring her to retreat. To run away. But she wouldn't. She was determined to do this. Why should she allow anything to stop her? She had forgotten what it was she was afraid of after all these years. Failure? Embarrassment? What did that matter now? How would she ever learn if she wasn't even prepared to try? Millions of people did this every day.

She picked up the article one more time:

There are no shortcuts for this giant of French classical cooking, but that doesn't mean it's not manageable. Each to their own – just as long as there's wine.

She took a deep breath, reached into the cupboard, pulled out her old apron and put it on. The boeuf bourguignon was certainly not going to make itself.

This time tomorrow, six people would be sitting down at her table expecting to be fed. She had invited Rachel, Karl, Josie and Helen round to meet Jon in person. School and work had finished for Christmas. At least in her house. It seemed as good a time as any.

Lizzy and Jack were going to their dad's. Or more accurately Ed's. Damien had moved in with his father when Ed came out of hospital. Both were recovering from what the last few months had thrown at them. In different ways, they needed each other.

Ed lived within walking distance of Sally's house and was always pleased to see his grandchildren. Damien being there too seemed to make things even simpler for them. They would visit whenever they felt like it rather than waiting for arrangements to be made. They still needed their father; despite the disaster he'd been as a husband.

The children had not seemed to mind Jon coming to the house these last few weeks. At least they hadn't said so. Most of the time they had just carried on as normal. Sometimes they even appeared to enjoy his company. His tales of television journalism were a good ice breaker, reducing their natural suspicions about this man in their mum's life.

286

Jon had not stayed overnight at hers yet, nor she at his. They wanted their children to get used to the idea of them simply being a couple before they added anything else to the mix. And after all her hurry a few months ago, their first time seemed too important for a quickie with their eyes on the time and the front door.

Sally checked the ingredients one more time. She had been shopping that morning but she wanted to be sure.

1 bottle of fruity, relatively light dry red wine
1 onion, peeled and cut into 6 wedges
1 large carrot, scrubbed and cut into 2cm chunks
2 garlic cloves, peeled and squashed with the back of a knife
1 bay leaf,
Small bunch of parsley, plus a handful for garnish
2 sprigs of thyme
2 tbsp olive oil
35g butter
200g unsmoked bacon lardons or a thick piece of unsmoked bacon cut into 2cm cubes
24 pearl onions, or 12 small shallots
18 baby carrots
200g button mushrooms
2 tbsp flour
1kg beef cheeks, cut into 3cm chunks
400g oxtail
60ml brandy
250ml good beef stock

Good. She had everything. It certainly wasn't a cheap meal. Had she aimed too high? She put the wine in a pan with the onion, carrot, garlic and herbs. She brought it to the boil and then put it on a low heat.

She looked again at the newspaper she had placed onto the worktop.

'Simmer for 30 minutes until reduced by about half'

Sally had no idea what that meant. How could you reduce something just by cooking it in a pan? She was almost pleased to be distracted by her phone.

Helen skipped the pleasantries.

"I've just been to the clinic and they think they've got their dates wrong. Some computer mix up. I'm due on Christmas Day."

Sally put the phone into her left hand and used the right to start heating her oven to 150^{0}C.

"Christmas Day? Next week? Are they sure?"

"Well as much as they can ever be. They said I'm really large to have three weeks left to go. There was someone else with same name. They might have accidentally confused our details."

The pot on the hob was boiling over. Sally moved it to a smaller ring.

"Well, you are all ready, aren't you Helen? And if you need me on Christmas Day, I'll be there. I won't be missed at my mum's. There's always a cast of thousands."

Helen audibly sighed. "Thanks Sally. What would I do without you? It all suddenly seems so real."
Sally heaved a large casserole dish out of the drawer. She put it on the worktop, ready for action.

"Don't worry about me. The only thing I've got on my plate right now is making sure you have something on yours tomorrow."

Helen gasped. "Tomorrow! Yes of course. I'm really looking forward to it!"

Sally could sense Helen was hurriedly checking the calendar on her wall. She questioned whether she should be serving her something based on wine. It was probably a moot point. And a small drop of burgundy might do the baby and its mother some good.

The oil and butter went into the casserole dish that had been placed over a medium-high heat. Sally was about to congratulate herself on her progress so far when the contents started reacting with each other in an alarming fashion. She checked the recipe.

'When the foam has died down, add the bacon'

It was normal. Thank goodness for that. But where was the bacon? She had forgotten to slice it into cubes. She was going to do that when Helen rang. She pulled open the packet. Who would know whether they were 2cms or not? Surely it couldn't matter that much? She threw cuts of bacon into the casserole dish and fried it. When it resembled something close to a golden colour, she scooped the bacon out with a slotted spoon and set it aside.

Just at that moment, Jack walked in. Sally immediately felt irritated by his presence and then just as quickly felt guilty.

"That smells good Mum. Is it for your meal tomorrow? Do you need any help?"

Sally looked around the kitchen. She had blamed Helen's call for the bacon not being ready. But she had failed to prepare anything in advance. Only the beef had been chopped and that had been done by the butcher. She had just thrown herself into it. Leapt before she looked. The words on the newspaper in front of her were starting to swirl in and out of focus. Perhaps her new-found confidence was all a delusion.

Jack had followed her eyes. "Feel the fear and do it anyway Mum! Isn't that what those books for old people say?"

Jack pulled a sharp knife out of the drawer, chopped the mushrooms and added them to the pan that had been simmering. He cooked them until they were lightly golden, then scooped them into a fresh bowl. Then he added the onions, turned down the heat slightly, and fried them until they were just beginning to brown. Sally put the flour on a plate, seasoned it, then rolled the beef in it. She added the onions to the other vegetables and turned up the heat slightly in the pan.

"Thank you so much, Jack. Where did all that talent come from?"

Jack looked sheepish.

"I've been cooking with Dad and Grandad. I was worried you wouldn't like it. I want to be a chef. You can train at college."

Sally gave her son a hug. Damien had at last done something constructive for his children. How could she mind that?

"That's fantastic. Can you finish this whole thing for me then?"

"Sorry Mum, I'm off out. Maybe next time."

Jack turned and fled before his mum had any chance to change his mind.

Sally started to fry the beef. It took a couple of attempts and some extra oil to work out just how big a batch needed to be to avoid boiling the juices. When they were *'crusted and deeply browned'* she scooped the beef out and put it in a bowl. She turned up the heat on the pan and added the brandy.

When she stirred, she noticed some bits of caramelised beef stuck on the bottom. She scraped the spoon against them. They soon dislodged. She checked the recipe again.

'Strain in the reduced wine'

Why did they have to keep writing in this language that was so foreign to her? Why had she not studied the recipe properly? Looking at it and reading it were two very different things.

"Mum, it's me," Sally said down the phone. "I'm sorry but I can't do conversation right now. I'm having a culinary crisis!"

"Oh dear, what's the matter?"

"What does 'strain the reduced wine' mean? It sounds like me and Josie trying to get the last dregs out of a Pinot Grigio!"

"Well, I don't know about that. As the wine simmers, there's less of it. It disappears in the steam and flavours the vegetables. Then you pour the wine through a sieve to separate the remaining liquid."

"In that case it sounds like bringing up the children!"

Sally did as she'd been told. She would need to ring her mum back and tell her she might not be there for Christmas Day. How well would she take that? It had been a white lie to say her absence would not be noticed. And who would get the children there? She returned the beef cheeks and oxtail to the pan and set it to simmer.

She was on the home straight now. Not much more left to do. Nearly everything was in the casserole dish. She put on the lid and placed it in the oven. She had two hours grace before she needed to tip in the onions, mushrooms and carrots and then bake for another thirty minutes.

She looked at the bottle of red wine that she'd used for the meal. There were a few drops left inside. She lifted it to her lips. Just in time for Lizzy to see her from the hall.

"Mum! What is the matter with you?"

Sally quickly assessed her mental state. What WAS the matter with her? She put the bottle down. Untouched.

"Nothing Lizzy. Nothing at all." She so wished that was true.

Three hours later, Sally scooped out the oxtail and stripped the meat from the bones before stirring it back into the pan with the bacon. There was just one more step to take.

'Season to taste'.

The next morning, Sally was up early to check on her masterpiece. She was in the kitchen when she heard a lorry rumbling loudly on the road. Bugger! She had forgotten they were coming today. There had been a flyer. Something to do with Christmas and Bank Holidays.

She was in her dressing gown. The bins were still by the front door. She had to pull them down the drive. So what if anyone saw her straight out of bed? No make-up. Hair as yet unbrushed. No one was looking. It was cold out there though. She rummaged in the shoe box in the hall for her black slip-ons. Where were they?

The only shoes in there seemed to belong to Jack and Lizzy. Neither had inherited Sally's small feet. Sod it! She would have to wear the felt, elf slippers she had bought for Lizzy last year that had been left out so long they were now appropriate again. In for a penny...

Sally opened the front door and stepped outside. She hadn't anticipated the chill wind. She pulled her dressing gown even tighter around her body and put her head down. Dragging the bins to the kerb was trickier than usual. It was a relief when a man in a high vis jacket took them from her and pushed them towards the truck.

"Damien?"

Her ex-husband opened his arms wide as if conceding defeat.

"Yes. It's me. Collecting your rubbish."

Sally's dressing gown was protecting her against what must have been a temperature of sub zero degrees. She folded her arms against her chest.

"Why? How?"

"Because I need a job. I used to work for Sharon's dad, if you remember. He 'suggested' I might want to resign after he found out about Laura and the twins."

"Why didn't the children tell me?"

"I asked them not to. I don't usually do your street. Not that there's anything wrong with this job. It's honest hard work. And quite well paid, actually. I just know what you're like."

That was unfair. Sally had never been a snob. But there WAS some irony in Damien taking away the things she no longer needed.

Damien rubbed the back of his gloved hand against his forehead.

"I'm glad you got back with that Jon. I felt guilty about the phone call."

"What phone call?"

"Didn't he tell you? I was sure he would have done."

"No. He didn't."

"After I turned up at your house. The next day. You were in the bath. Jon called. I told him to back off. For the sake of our family. I said we were trying again. That's why he sent you the note."

A flash of anger crossed Sally's brain. Then it stopped. Sharply. It didn't matter anymore. None of this mattered anymore. She had learnt from the past and let go.

"I'm starting afresh Damien. You should too. Maybe this time we can get it right."

Back in the house, she put the potatoes onto boil. Then she returned the casserole to the oven to slowly re-heat. She couldn't find the parsley. She had definitely bought some. She seemed to have tidied it away the night before. She lifted a magazine off the kitchen table and there it was, squashed but still useable.

She went upstairs. Both children were awake and on their phones. They were due at Ed's in an hour, staying the night for the first time since his stroke.

Normally she would have nagged them but she wanted the bathroom to herself. Jack would do his usual trick of getting up with five minutes to go, Lizzy would have to finish her tortuously long morning routine when she got there.

As she washed and dressed her offspring stirred. How was it that they nearly always demanded to be left alone and then wanted so much of her attention when they were? No, she did not know why the internet wasn't working and she had not seen that pink scrunchy of which her daughter was so fond.

Admitting defeat, she turned the router on and off. Jack was supposed to be the computer expert. And she pulled the hair accessory out of the laundry basket where it had got caught up in a top Lizzy had worn the day before. With some cajoling, she bundled them out of the door and into the winter air.

She just had time to get dressed before the doorbell rang. What had they forgotten now? Sally looked down the hall. She could make out one adult silhouette against the frame. Josie breezed through the door as soon as Sally opened it.

"Morning! Thought you might need some help. Wow. Something smells good."

In an hour's time her home would be full. She and her friends would be sitting down to a meal she had cooked. From scratch. The food might be ready but she had not tidied the kitchen from this morning's labours, or vacuumed, as she'd planned.

"Thanks. You could clean the house."

Josie put a bottle of red on the work top.

"I was thinking something a bit less strenuous."

"In that case, it's all in hand."

"Really? Where's Sally and what have you done with her?"

"Very funny. I did it most of it yesterday. I just have to mash the potatoes when they're ready."

Josie looked around. As if she was searching for something that Sally might have forgotten.

"I'm impressed. Good on you."

"Thank you." Sally was impressed with herself too.

"Well, I'll disappear and come back again then," said Josie. "You can have a few minutes with Jon before we all descend on you. When are you expecting him?"

"In about ten minutes. But you don't need to go. You can keep him occupied while I do my last-minute stressing."

Josie looked pleased. She relaxed into one of the kitchen chairs.

"Actually, there was something I was going to tell you. Now seems as good a time as any."

The bell rang again.

Jon came in carrying more wine and some chocolates. He gave Sally a quick kiss on the lips. Josie pretended to cover her eyes. Jon blushed. He put his hand out.

"Hello... Josie?"

Josie brushed his arm away and gave him a welcoming hug.

"You've been in my living room every night for the last ten years. Surely we've gone past the handshake."

Jon hugged Josie back before turning his attention to Sally. "Smell's great. Would you like help laying the table?"

The table! Sally had completely forgotten about that. She ran around searching for a clean tablecloth while Josie checked the state of the glasses and cutlery. Jon was at the end of the production line, setting six places.

By the time Rachel and Karl arrived, they were ready. Her neighbours were followed in by Helen, slowly waddling up the path behind them.

Sally was surprised by how quickly they were all seated. She was relieved at how much they were eating. She was touched by how well they all seemed to get on.

It could be a strange combination of comforting and awkward when friends from different parts of your life came together in one place, usually for birthdays, weddings or funerals. They saw and liked different parts of the person that made the whole you, requiring all those parts to be present at once. Today, she felt at ease. Everything seemed to be slotting into place.

She looked around the table. Jon was 'interviewing' Rachel and Karl about how their lives had changed since Laura and the twins had moved out.

Soon after Damien was revealed as the father, Laura had packed their belongings and taken the three of them to Josie's across the road. Andrew had not gone back to university and was going to apply again, somewhere nearer to home, next year. The two were on their way to becoming a couple, with Laura using his support and college childcare to pick up her studies.

Sally could not really hear what Rachel was saying. But she already knew. Although they still saw them often, it was not the same. Rachel was missing the twins badly. Karl was keen for her to join him on a series of small adventures, now they had more time and less responsibility. Top of his list was a trip to Egypt to see the pyramids. Karl might have more success if he suggested a tour of Devon in a campervan.

Both were agreed that Laura had done the right thing by taking on her responsibilities, even if they were less as one about the benefits of her and the twins living at Josie's in order to do so.

Josie was talking to Helen. Sally noticed that both were looking radiant. As if they were expecting something exciting to happen very soon. Of course, in Helen's case it was obvious what that was. Josie was more of a mystery. Sally leaned in to listen.

She had to pay particular attention when Helen spoke, as her bump meant she was further away from the table than normal. She could only catch some of her words. "...a doctor at the hospital. It's early days ...already seen more of me than you might expect ...before we've even gone on a date!"

This was news to Sally. Why had Helen not told her about this doctor? Why couldn't she talk a bit louder? Fortunately, Josie was easier to hear. "The house is very full now. Tomorrow..."

Without warning, Helen stood up from the table. Her chair fell onto the wooden floor behind her with a loud bang. Everyone jumped.

Sally spoke first.

"Are you ok?"

Helen shook her head. Then nodded.

"My waters just broke!"

Dinner was forgotten. Offers to drive to the hospital were quickly followed by confessions of alcohol intake. An ambulance was called. Sally travelled with Helen, leaving her guests behind. It was the first time she had been in an emergency vehicle with its blue lights in flashing; the road clearing in front of them.

An hour later Helen was lying on a bed in a labour room. The midwife had been and gone several times already.

"I'm scared," said Helen.

"You'll be fine," Sally replied, taking Helen's hand. "Lots of women have done it before."

"Not of giving birth. I'm scared I won't be as good as you. At doing it alone."

Sally winced as her hand was gripped harder than she might have liked.

"I've never been alone," she said. Understanding, for the first time, just how true that was.

Sally remembered something from dinner. "What's this about you and a doctor?"

"How did you hear that? I've only told Josie. Oh, I get it. My, what big ears you have Grandmama."

"Just spill the beans."

"It's my GP. We seem to have hit it off. She likes me and I like her."

"She? Her?"

"Yes. That's right. She. There's more than one reason why I'm doing this alone."

"But we've been friends for years. Why am I only being told this now?"

"Because I only admitted it to myself a year ago. And it's not like I'd met someone. I just had to finally be true to myself. For now, could you get someone? I think I'm having a baby."

The midwife returned and went to the bottom of the bed.

"I just need to check how dilated you are, Mum." She looked up.

"Right, look at me and push when your body tells you."

Sally appreciated why Helen had not wanted her mum at the birth. The baby arriving in Room Three at Second City Hospital was greeted with a flow of words that would have made a sailor blush.

The new born infant was placed Helen's arms. It was beautiful to see. Then the baby was taken away to be checked, before being wrapped in a hospital sheet, under the yellow blanket Sally had given her friend as a gift.

When the midwife offered Helen tea and toast, Sally became acutely aware she was very hungry. She had hardly touched her meal before the drama had begun. She kissed Helen on the top of her head.

"Well done you."

Helen looked up, her eyes glistening with joy.

"Thank you. For everything."

"You did it all," said Sally, who was now just as tired as she was famished.

Helen shook head.

"I started my new life, this new life, because of you. Now I've interrupted yours. I'm fine. We're fine. I'll still be here tomorrow. Go home and make things happen."

Sally walked into the main maternity wing. She WAS keen to get home. But first she needed to eat. She looked at the overhead signs, searching for the canteen. She saw Josie at the very last minute as her friend jumped up from one of the nearby chairs.

"It's a girl!" Sally answered the silent question. "She's gorgeous."

"Oh fantastic," said Josie. "I'm so pleased."

Josie put her arms around Sally in a celebratory hug.

"I thought you might need a lift,"

Sally tried to remember where she'd left her car. At home. She had come in the ambulance!

They walked to the far end of the hospital car park in near silence. Sally paused as she watched Josie press a button on her keys and the lights of her vehicle just up ahead of them flashed on and off.

"Thanks Josie. What would I do without you?"

"You'll be fine."

Josie seemed preoccupied, pulling away fast as Sally still struggled with her seatbelt. She slowed down, nearly to a stop, as she approached the junction onto the main road.

"There's another reason I came."

"What do you mean?"

"I was trying to tell you before. I'm going traveling for six months. I leave tomorrow."

Sally struggled to take in this new information. There had been so much information, if not food, to digest that day already.

"Where are you going? What about your job? The house?"

"Everywhere. Anywhere. I've given up my job. I've got savings. Andrew and Laura can play happy families. You've taught me something Sally. Life is a lottery and sometimes we have to take a gamble. Not playing means we avoid the £10 disappointments, but we also deny ourselves the chance of winning the big prizes."

"Why didn't you tell me?"

"I was scared I might not go through with it."

Sally spent the rest of the journey questioning her friend. Josie had stayed in touch with George's shipmate Stephen. He was single and had access to cruise discounts. And he had offered them to Josie. She had said yes. The next day, she was getting on a cruise from Southampton to Norway. With Stephen on the crew. She was happier than Sally had ever seen her. They parted with a long hug. It was the end and start of something

Sally let herself into the house and slumped down on the sofa without turning on the light. She could just make out the hands on the big clock telling her it was 10pm. She was exhausted but she could not rest yet. Her hunger had still not been satisfied.

She could hear someone in the kitchen. That couldn't be right. She had expected the house to be empty. The door into the living room opened, chasing the darkness out.

She spoke first. "You're still here?"

Jon waved the tea towel he was holding. "I couldn't leave you to clear up a mess you didn't make. What's the news?"

"A healthy baby girl," said Sally.

"That's great."

Jon sat down next to Sally and put his arm around her shoulders. She felt safe and content.

"I'm afraid we ate all the casserole."

There was a comfortable silence. Each breathing in the other's presence.

Jon gently held her face in his hands. His eyes sparkling in anticipation.

"What happens now?" he said.

Sally paused, savouring this moment.

"There's always dessert."

Keep in Touch:

Facebook @thejoyofjarsbook

Twitter: @joannebarker

Instagram: @thejoyofjars

Email: thejoyofjars@gmail.com

Thejoyofjars.wordpress.com

Printed in Great Britain
by Amazon